Arms
FROM THE
SEA

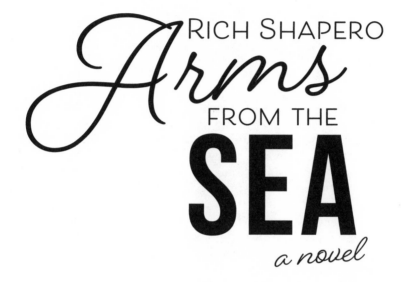

RICH SHAPERO

Arms

FROM THE

SEA

a novel

TooFar
MEDIA

HALF MOON BAY, CALIFORNIA

TooFar Media
500 Stone Pine Road, Box 3169
Half Moon Bay, CA 94019

Library of Congress Cataloging-in-Publication Data is available.

ISBN-13: 978-0-9718801-7-7

Cover painting by Eugene Von Bruenchenhein
(for more information, visit www.VonBruenchenhein.com)
Artwork copyright © 2009 Rich Shapero
Additional graphics: Sky Shapero
Cover design: Adde Russell

Printed in the United States of America

20 19 18 17   2 3 4 5 6

Also by Rich Shapero

The Hope We Seek

Too Far

Wild Animus

1 A Living Wheel

The chambers of Fossil Wells. Moonlight and thick shadow allowed Lyle to imagine them as they once were. Water's power had been preserved there, incised where streams whirled potholes, hollowed into caverns as the gorge opened up and the currents drilled deeper. The Wells were rock salt, and from the bedded strata of its pockets a myriad creatures hailed and beckoned, as if expecting some observer from the future to return them to life.

A man of twenty-six years, he was wiry with a round head and hair stiff as straw. He stood on a ledge of the east wall. Because the gorge ran through city center, the tops of tall buildings were visible. He couldn't see the patrols, but a streamer of salt dust glittered in the moonlight, marking their presence around the construction on the west rim of the gorge. Here, amid the ruins of the east wall, Lyle was alone.

The wells around him had been blasted and cleared. The jagged lips and shattered shells looked like so many broken pots fallen off a supply transport. He shut the loss out of his mind, facing a spot he remembered—directly opposite—with a perfect white bowl. He imagined he was curled inside it, dreaming of the ancient sea. The night sky was clear, but he drew clouds across it, combers that roiled like waves above him. And when he closed his eyes, the currents caught him. He was doubled and tumbling, senseless and breathless, immersed in the swarm of unusual lives, embraced in kinship by the primeval rivers.

He parted his lids, and through the part he could see the rear wall of the white bowl, its hardened shell like the skull of some alien mind. A mind that dreamt and created, nourished and sustained; the mind that conceived of the boundless ocean and filled its unfailing currents.

His loyalty was to that eternal blue, however distant and vague. His time here in the desert— Perhaps it was right that it should end.

Lyle drew a breath and turned, finding hand grips and footholds in the shattered wall, climbing out of the Wells. His hands were large and his legs were strong, and the speed of his ascent showed the skill of one who'd spent years among the salt cliffs. His temperament was impulsive, but his movements were measured and deliberate, as if they'd been learned in a medium denser than air.

As he rose onto the east rim, he checked the pathway and the white buildings opposite, pale eyes darting, lips trembling, coughing and brushing his yellow hair aside. He opened his backpack, retrieved a mask and drew it over his face: a grinning corpse. Then he turned and hurried toward the pathway.

Along a white street, white vehicles droned. Their headlights rayed through the salt spicules. Lyle was hidden in the dimness, but as he turned, the moon shone on a withered cheek and nose. The corpse face scanned the thoroughfare. The traffic was thin. He removed a metal cylinder from his pack and held it to his nape, scrambling the tuner. Twenty minutes, at most. Here, at city center, tracers would recover his vectors quickly. He turned and gripped the crusted bars, salt crystals squealing in his fists, and mounted the white gate. Ten feet to its spikes and over, dropping to the ground on the far side. Then across the saltstone pavers of the park grounds.

The memorial towered over him, stark white beneath the moon and the spotlight beams, its blades and bands glittering, the long facets of the tapering spire flashing as he approached. In the shadows, hugging its pediment, Lyle clipped into the rope coiled on his shoulder. Not a moment wasted—

His hands were on the rock salt. He was ascending.

He angled across the base, using weather pits for toeholds, securing his hands in cracks and on nubs. Ten feet up, he reached a ragged sill with a line of repeated symbols—stylized limbs, clasped in fellowship. Above, pairs of tall tablets like shuttered windows. Through the holes in his mask, his lips were tense, his eyes like embers blown from coals. He pulled the hammer from his waistband and found a piton in his pocket. *Tap, tap.* The salt-covered spike sank into the memorial, and he resumed the climb, following a groove between casements.

His frame was thin, but his legs were sure and his arms banded with muscle. He moved carefully, jambing knees and elbows, and when he was eye level with the tablet tops, he put in another spike. It was past midnight, but the air was stifling. Beneath the jaw of his mask, a rill of sweat descended, darkening the salt that powdered his neck. Below, the white courtyard surrounding the memorial extended on all sides, and beyond the grounds, a labyrinth of pale roads and bleached buildings. White vehicles, white sanctuaries with people in them, sealed behind glass, their faces rigid and cracked, dusted with chalk.

Lyle surmounted a row of open eyes, carved by craftsmen before he was born. Below a second tier of tablets he put in another anchor. And as he topped those, a sill carved with starbursts came into view, symbols of liberated understanding. The people who chiseled this were a simple lot, and trusting.

He paused on the sill and put in another spike. *Tap, tap.*

Two guards crossed the front court. Lyle froze. Had they heard him? Were they responding to a signaling device he'd tripped without knowing? They panned strobe lights across the base of the tower. And now the strobes ran up it, pausing at the top. Lyle held his breath. A moment later the lights were doused. He could hear the guards muttering, reporting

4

through their tuners. Steps. They were moving again, disappearing into the shadows.

His relief was mixed with anger. He turned away as from something insufferable, pulling his fingers to limber them. The sill carved with starbursts circled the memorial like a starched skirt. To delay was foolhardy, but emotion forced him: he looked out over the roofs of the city to the ridges rising in the distance. White, all white. The encrusted warrens, the nameless flats, the mountain walls— A dead world, as far as the eye could see. He scanned the southern edge of the urban labyrinth. There, beyond a confusion of cranes and scaffolding, were the paths of his childhood. A ruined shack. And inside, those to whom he owed life. A helpless mother with a runneled face and a crooked hand. Somehow the uncertain boy she loved had become an enemy of the State.

Lyle shifted his feet on the sill and faced the heights. Pinnacles were clustered around the central spire. He squeezed between two, finding toeholds and handholds, moving through the spotlight beams, rising slowly with the moon behind him like some hero from mythology, approaching the spire and its imposing statue.

He was bridging the gap, scrabbling at the steeple's base, hunched like a malcontent gargoyle determined to perch on a higher place. He straightened and started up it, clinging—

The spire was studded with cubes and pyramids. He gripped them, climbing without protection, approaching the globe at its top. The father of the State stood thirty feet tall, facing the stars, his sandals on the sphere. Glittering and rigid,

5

he posed for the generations, imagining himself the pride of his people.

Lyle reached the globe and muscled over it, getting his hand on one of the patriarch's feet. His arms circled the giant's ankle.

Up, under the statue's right side, feeling over the planes and curves, working around his front. Lyle inched up his pant leg, hugging the calf, planting a foot on a fold at his knee. The patriarch's hand was raised, addressing the multitudes. The difference in size struck Lyle powerfully. The grip of Salt had withstood the centuries, the passing of oceans, the joining of continents. Did he think he could change that?

He drew his right arm back and hammered a bolt into the patriarch's groin, very much in view now. He scanned the streets below. No one seemed to be watching, but there were undoubtedly sensors— Were alarms already sounding?

No fear, no hesitation—

Lyle moved up the patriarch's front, gripping folds in his sweater, finding footholds on his belt. *Clumsy job*, he rated the sculpting. The carvers had aimed at spartan dignity, but the result was homely and crude. Who was he really, this author of the First Liberation? A man of passion and conviction, a man who felt fear and gambled his life. A great fool, but a brave one.

Lyle put a bolt in his sternum. The ringing of his hammer shattered the silence. He shifted his gaze to the quiet city and back, then boosted himself onto the statue's bicep, straddling his shoulder and scooting along it.

Closer, closer—

Lyle rose beneath his chin, standing in midair at the top of the memorial. A step forward, and another—

The corner of the great mouth was turned up, the nostrils flared. His expression was stern, as if he could hear Lyle or smell him. The sculpted eyes glared as Lyle raised his hammer and drove a spike into his lip, above the eyetooth. And then—

Salt flew as Lyle battered his visage. Pocks at first. A pit in his cheek. The lower lip sagged and the smirk faded. Then the end of his nose and an eye—Lyle's hammer made quick work of it, leaving nothing but an empty socket.

Pieces rained onto the courtyard below. As Lyle started on the other eye, voices reached him.

Trouble.

The sound of footfalls on the pavers. Arc lights, many of them, swept over the patriarch's backside. Lyle paused, hammer drawn back. On the street, vehicles were pulling over. People got out—no uniforms, just Citizens in loose pants and smocks. Across the way, on the third floor, a couple at the window faced the statue, pointing.

On the other side of the park, men in white uniforms appeared, sprinting around a dead fountain, hurrying toward the memorial. The patriarch's front was visible to them, lit by the floods. Across the way, windows had opened. The couple was shouting down to the street. Crowds were gathering around the park's perimeter, faces lined the grating, staring up at the father of the State and the small figure standing on his shoulder.

The moment Lyle had feared.

"Avoiding detection will be difficult," the leader of Solution had said earlier that evening. The insurgents thought he was mad. All they saw was his privilege. They didn't understand how he'd been betrayed. How he'd been left with no choice but to barter away everything that mattered to him.

A siren started up close by—the sound of Helpers roused to action. Others joined it in quick succession, as if the metropolis itself was wounded and howling from all its precincts.

"Citizen El-mu-zero-five-nine-delta—" A robotic voice sounded in his head. Lyle touched the spot above his nape where the tuner was implanted. "You have entered a restricted area," she said. "Your actions are unlawful. Remain motionless. An advisor will be with you shortly."

They couldn't see what he saw or hear what he was thinking. But he was no longer scrambled. They knew who he was and what he was doing. And that was the end of it.

There would be no forbearance. No more reprieves.

Lyle removed his mask and let a warm breeze take it. In the spotlights, his dripping face was like a cornered beast's, eyes burning, his blond shocks crushed like weeds. He bucked his head with contempt and tried to smile. The State of Salt would be shaken. In every twist of the urban labyrinth, lights were igniting. People would ask why, and the answers—

None of that mattered. His dream was intact. Defiance protected it. The vision of a sea change was roaring inside him, and there was nothing they could do—now or ever—to take it away.

A ghostly voice echoed through the streets. Speaking through every tuner, the Helper broadcast resounded like the voice of the patriarch himself. An unprovoked crime, the voice said, motive unknown; reassurance the offenders will be caught, directions to secure the public well-being. At the end of the boulevard bordering the park, a platoon appeared.

Lyle's hands were powdered white. Salt crusted his nostrils and circled his lips. He affected a snarl, but what he felt now was nausea and shivering dismay. He was thinking of what remained, of the action he had to take.

"Citizen El-mu-zero-five-nine-delta—" The robot repeated her warning as the platoon marched through the gate, white soldiers in ranks. Armored vehicles were descending on the park from every angle of the city. Transports, paralysis screens, tankers of myelin smoke and swivel-neck launchers. White machines, white armies, white poison—

Lyle found another piton and hammered it into the remains of the patriarch's ear. He dipped his left hand into his smock and retrieved a carved figurine—an imaginary creature with a tube body, looping antennae and a ring of eyes—and he hung the figure on the piton. Then his arm went slack and the tool fell from his hand.

Would there be an upheaval, now or ever? Perhaps the only one possible was in the mind of a misfit, a disconnected soul. For this one, the struggle was over.

His hand returned to his pocket and found what Solution had given him.

Lyle opened his fingers and watched the capsule roll in his

palm, sapphire blue in the pitiless glare. It was time to pour petroleen on himself and strike a match. Time to jump off the edge of the world.

~~~

Earlier that evening, Lyle had requested a meeting with Solution. When the request was granted, he made his way to the shelter on the salt flats beyond the city's perimeter. The location was out of Helper range, but they scrambled his tuner for safety. Red One, Solution head, was astonished to see him. The damage Lyle did at Helper HQ was public knowledge. How had he gotten his freedom? Some were suspicious, but Red One was convinced he hadn't been turned. No rebel was more rabid than the young sculptor.

Lyle explained what he planned to do. Red One pointed up the dangers and tried to dissuade him. Defacing the statue would disrupt the city, but would it trigger hostilities? He agreed Lyle's notoriety had reached a new level, but Solution wasn't ready to launch an offensive. "You'll never be ready," Lyle fumed. The insurgents could see he was distraught. They shared a hatred for Salt, but when Lyle spouted his litany of the sea, he lost them completely.

"We're cut off from our source," he railed. "Beached, baked— This life, our essence—" He clawed his chest. "It's dying inside us."

Empty stares. When Red One's deputy rolled his eyes, the leader shot him an angry look.

"End the State," Lyle urged them. "Sweep it away. Starting tonight." Even as he spoke, he was conscious of the gulf that separated his passion for a revolution in spirit from the changes in government that motivated Solution.

"Avoiding detection will be difficult," Red One said.

Lyle shook his head, unwilling to think about that. Defiance was everything. He wasn't going to let himself be a pawn of the State.

Red One dismissed the group. "Bring Clean-Cut in here," he ordered. "And the film of his Expiation."

"None of them understand. Not a one," Lyle motioned angrily, taking in the insurgents, the First City and the far-flung empire of Salt.

"To force an appreciation for your sea would require a regime as oppressive as the one we suffer under now." Red One drew a breath. "You know what will happen if they catch you."

"They won't," Lyle said.

"Being in the public eye has consequences."

A lieutenant led in Clean-Cut, the charismatic leader of Solution who preceded Red One. Lyle was familiar with him and knew his story, but the sight was disturbing nonetheless. The man's face was crossed by jagged seams, like a badly sewn quilt.

The lieutenant set a screen on the desk, and at a nod from Red One he played the broadcast that had been viewed by every adult and school-age child in the State.

"An atrocity," Lyle said weakly, sensitive to Clean-Cut's presence. He remembered the broadcast. Who could forget it?

The video showed the former leader sitting in a hospital bed, face newly disfigured. A doctor was with him, a tall woman with blond hair, who Lyle knew only too well. She slid her hand into her white coat and eyed the camera, explaining the State's policy of fiat mutilation for dissidents. And then Clean-Cut spoke, confessing his crimes, disavowing his cohorts and pleading for mercy. Lyle's reaction to the broadcast was no different than anyone else's. It was obvious the Expiation was obtained under duress, and it was probably doctored. But between the gruesome punishment and Clean-Cut's apparent submission, the State's intolerance for rebellion was clearly communicated.

"I was foolish, arrogant," Clean-Cut said to the camera. "I ask for the Citizens' forgiveness," he turned to Doctor Wentt, "and the Helpers' mercy."

Red One gestured and the lieutenant stopped the film. Clean-Cut bowed his head.

"He didn't say that," Lyle sighed.

"No, he didn't," Red One said. "All they needed was raw footage. The rest was edits and overdubs. We lost half our outfit. It killed recruiting for three years."

Clean-Cut's humiliation filled the room.

Red One motioned for the lieutenant to leave.

"When you were nobody, you didn't matter," Red One said. "But now—" He nodded at the video screen. "That's how they'd use you."

"I would have chosen death," Clean-Cut said.

"You want to bring down the State—" Red One peered at Lyle. He shifted his gaze to the disfigured man, as if to show Lyle what failure looked like. "Talk to him. You should know what he went through."

With that, Red One exited the room.

Lyle listened as Clean-Cut described his grisly ordeal: the incarceration, the medicines, the conditions under which the incisions were made and the questioning that followed. When they'd finished, Red One returned.

"Well?"

"I'm going to do it," Lyle said.

"Give me a week or two," Red One suggested. "Ask the Minister to give you more time."

Lyle shook his head. "He can't."

Red One regarded him gravely.

"You've got your scrambler?" he asked.

Lyle nodded.

The leader led him to a utility closet. "For the security cameras," he said. He opened the door, and Lyle selected a mask from those hanging there.

"Give me your hand," Red One said.

When Lyle extended it, Red One turned it palm up and placed the capsule in it.

"If I can muster a resistance," the leader said, "we'll be with you." He grabbed Lyle's shoulders and shook him.

The capsule glittered in Lyle's palm. He took it between his thumb and forefinger, raising it slowly.

Military vehicles had reached the boulevard below.

Lyle admired the sapphire hue and coruscating reflections, turning the capsule before him. Then he parted his lips and placed it on his tongue.

His hands shook as he knotted the climbing rope and clipped himself to the bolt in the patriarch's face. An involuntary sob, and then his stumbling gaze found its way along a fence of buildings, down the dim boulevard to the dark declivity of Fossil Wells. He imagined he was curled in a favorite chamber, hearing and feeling the ancient currents. He was feverish, delirious. Creatures drifted by, noticing, pausing, fanning fins, flexing appendages. They were swarming around him, ready to accompany him on the journey he was about to make.

He mastered his quivering jaw and bit down, cracking the capsule.

A cold wave expanded from Lyle's mouth, staining his mind midnight blue. Amid the blue, a burst of light—an exploding hub with reaching spokes, spiraling open, turning and turning. Arms red at the center, blue where their urgency pierced the night—a living wheel with numberless arms, all-consuming.

Was this death taking control? Or a glowing call to return to life?

The arms of the wheel reached for Lyle, crossing the boundary between the two.

2 Behold the Sea

The rumble of transports was mounting. There were more soldiers in the street than at a Liberation Day parade.

Lyle's mystic wheel had dissolved. Beneath him, they had opened the gates of the park and the tankers and launchers were rumbling through, rolling up before a squad of men donning metalized suits. Sedans followed, circling the troops and military vehicles. They screeched to a halt, intelligence agents and State reporters piling out. From the largest, a man in night togs emerged.

The sight amused Lyle. It wasn't the Minister's habit to attend to State business in his bathrobe. Jordan was with him. The young soldier had managed to pull on his coat and pants. Flanked by Jordan and a half-dozen aides, the Minister strode toward the troop commander. The two were directly below now, at the foot of the memorial, conferring. Minister Audrie put a finger to his ear and lifted his chin, staring up.

"Lyle—" His voice crackled through Lyle's tuner. "What is this? You've done it now." His practiced calm was gone, his tone harsh. "Some thanks. Damn you. Drown you!"

No Citizens were listening. They were on a closed channel, their words heard only by Helpers.

"Thanks?" Lyle said. "For a thirty-year sentence."

"That was your doing," Audrie snapped. "If you'd only—"

"You were lying to me." Lyle said the words slowly, sadly.

"I was your patron, you fool."

"You were using me. From the very first day."

"You had nothing," Audrie said. "Your talent was wasted."

"That blab about giving Salt a new soul—" Lyle faltered. "You didn't care about my creatures."

"No, I didn't," the Minister admitted. "Any more than you cared about my people. No one in Salt wants your sea, Lyle. Can't you accept that?"

Lyle heard Audrie's sigh through his tuner.

"There were things we could have done," the Minister said. "You could have left your mark—"

"All you care about is power," Lyle told him. "I won't be used. By any of you," he added for the Helpers listening in. Then to Audrie, "Your day is over. The Chief will strip you and move you to Sewage."

Audrie laughed. "You're a sneeze to me, Lyle. I'll blow my nose and forget you."

A runner was cleared through the gate. He raced toward the Minister.

Audrie turned aside, closing the circuit to speak to him. When they'd finished, he reopened the channel. "It's your mother. She's passed. Before this humiliation, thankfully."

Lyle felt like he'd been struck. He reached for the rope as if to steady himself, picturing her motionless on the bed, father seated beside her, despairing.

"A timely send-off," Audrie said acidly, "from your only child. You still have your rights." His voice was hard as stone. "There's some chance of lenience if you—"

"No more bargains," Lyle screamed.

The Minister dodged his head and put his hand to his ear. Lyle saw nothing. His vision was blurred, eyes narrowed and searching. As if he might find her, alive and conscious. Conscious enough to hear him say goodbye.

Traffic on the street was parting. The cordon by the park gates relaxed to admit a second convoy of sedans and military vehicles. Doors opened and more officials and soldiers stepped out. Doctor Wentt was among them. She strode up to Audrie and after a brief exchange, she raised her arm and pointed toward the Minister's car. He headed for it with Jordan at his rear, and a moment later, they disappeared inside.

Lyle heard a click in his tuner, and Wentt turned to face him. She wore a black dress with a red scarf, and her stance was straight as a chisel. The eyes of the Helpers had all shifted to her.

"Will you come down from there?" Wentt asked him.

Her voice was calm, her manner unhurried.

Lyle didn't answer.

17

"That's good enough for me," she said with finality. Wentt raised her arm and waved the troop commander forward, and the gears of the State engaged. The commander barked an order. A unit of soldiers wearing gas masks and headlamps marched forward. They carried ropes and climbing equipment. Another order from the troop commander, and the neck of a nearby launcher swiveled toward the statue. A drone sounded over the hubbub as the barrel telescoped out.

They expected resistance, but retrieving him would be easier than that. All they would need was a van for his body. By the time they reached him, he would be gone. Lyle sensed it now—the drug in the capsule was working.

His balance wavered. The air popped in his ears. He felt weightless, unsubstantial. If he unclipped from the statue, he might float away on the wind.

Lyle closed his eyes. In a few more moments, the nightmare of Salt would be over. He heard the spoken directives below, the shuffle of boots. A scrabbling of hands and feet and the clink of hardware as the masked climbers started up the memorial. No need to watch. He was an artist. From the sounds, he could fill out the scene.

Crack. He pictured a puff rising from the muzzle of the launcher. The first bomb of myelin smoke burst over him, billowing like an aureole around the head of the patriarch. The precepts of power set down in those days said nothing about weapons like these or crimes that wounded the pride of the State. But every culture has its trajectory.

A faint *whir.* From a distance.

Aircraft perhaps? Or an effect of the drug. A soundtrack for dying.

The whir pulsed, swelling and fading, like a resonating membrane in Lyle's head responding to some distant flux. Or a hidden pocket of fluid, trembling with communicated vibration. Perhaps the sound had always been there—like the high-pitched twinkling when you sink your head in calm water, or the stirring in the gel of your eye when you fix on the sun. There was energy in the sound—speed and motion. And detail, like a drop seen under a microscope, teeming with translucent protozoans.

Or—the sound was a memory. Perhaps he was hearing with an ancient ear, the ear of a forebear that swam the primordial seas. The currents still echoed in a hidden chamber of his brain. He was heir to them, feeling their rhythm as surely as the beat of his heart.

The sound of great waters.

Lyle thought, *I'm going home.*

He opened his eyes. The whir was suddenly louder. In the distance he saw what looked like a giant wave, moonlight caught on its crest. B_____ ___ _____, p____g ing in an unbroken arc. A fog rose where it landed, and cascades broke loose, silvering the foothills. Water raged down the slopes, crashed onto the valley floor and charged across the salt flats, furious, unstoppable. A wall of water roofed with froth—was it twenty feet high, a hundred?

Lyle felt a moment's hurrah, as if some idle wish had been granted in a waking dream. And then— Shock.

He wasn't dreaming.

The water was descending on him. On his city, his world.

The dark wall advanced rapidly, drowning the basin—

No one saw it. White soldiers scurried below like a horde of ants intent on their business.

Lyle swung his arm toward the wave, motioning frantically. The liquid cliff reached the city's edge and fell in a great curl, its scoop lined with foam, its crown bristling with fountains. Spray irised in the moonlight, dressing the comber in rainbow hues. The impact was like bombs going off, and the outer precincts vanished in the blast.

The roar echoed inside him, a horror-filled hollow brimming with bodies. Death, death for so many. Beneath islets of flying foam, currents tumbled and ripped, reaching from the whorls of vapor, swarming over each other, headed straight for his birthplace. In an instant, the angry deluge swallowed it. Mother, father—

The soldiers finally heard it, the white ants froze in their tracks. A roar and a hissing, the sound of pressure released. Lyle saw what they couldn't—the swath of ruin, houses dashed to pieces, buildings uprooted, spinning and dragged down. The flood was boiling through the City of Salt, racing for the park at its center.

Schoolmates, friends, children in bed, Red One and Clean-Cut and the Museum director. Lyle saw their faces as the water struck them. It was the end for them all.

The sirens died quickly, one after another. The ghostly voice of the broadcast alert was muffled and gagged. Doctor

Wentt stood in her black dress, turning her head. The couple on the third floor were wide-eyed, shouting into their tuners. Would they have time to explain? No, it was happening *right now*.

Between the tall buildings, giant windrows appeared. The buildings tipped and swayed and were torn from their foundations. The flood crashed through the park grating, rushing upon the platoons and vehicles, swallowing everything. The crowds circling the park were engulfed, roiled together with the soldiers and machines of the State, vanishing in the churn.

Lyle was choked with dread, clinging to his anchor, shaking in every part. A high-rise rolled past like a log, frantic faces in windows, pleading, trying to escape. Another—panes shattered, bodies emerging—broached a wave and was sucked under. A naked woman clinging to a bedframe gazed up at him, shocked, staring— Screams from rooftops, bobbing heads, cries from the rafting debris. Cries for a halt. But everything was in motion.

On the racing tide, an image was superimposed, rising unbidden. Lyle saw his mother in a silver gondola staring up at the sky. His father was seated beside her, holding her hand, scanning the melee for a glimpse of his son.

Beyond the park, the deluge rolled on, swamping what remained of the city. On a hill to the north, the Helper stronghold— An arm of the flow hooked and rose around it, crushing it like an empty carton. The waters had drowned the memorial's pediment and lower casements, and they were rising quickly, swallowing the limbs of fellowship, the open eyes, the starbursts of wisdom. The statue trembled beneath Lyle's feet. As he watched, the currents reached the masked climbers and tore them from their holds.

Cascades were still plunging through the pass. The inland lake continued to grow, its wave fronts moving toward the distant range. The last siren in the city was silenced. On every side, deep funnels whirled, dragging buildings and debris and people down—spiral eddies with foam tracers, like the turning thoughts of an alien mind. Beneath the surface, the currents were writhing and twisting in untold combinations.

Cold spray spattered Lyle's front and prickled his face. The waters had reached the top of the steeple. The globe bobbed like a buoy, and the next moment the statue's sandals were soaked. The father of the State stood on his ankles, his knees—And then—

The increase slowed.

The funnels flattened.

Lyle watched, mistrustful. Was the flooding over? The city and its people had vanished, and as the minutes crept by, the night grew still. Beneath the moon, the water extended in a continuous sheet, like molten silver.

It had found its level.

Lyle clung to his anchor, turning full around, taking in what the sea had done. All that remained were the peaks in the distance, a derelict statue sunk to its groin— And one living soul clipped to its head.

Exhaustion overcame him. When Lyle revived, the sky was paling. A glow was visible behind the mountains in the east. Around him, on every side—the sea.

It spread like a kaleidoscope fabric, emerald and blue, teal and chartreuse and aquamarine, with knots of froth woven through it—silver knots that tied and untied as he watched. Other than the darts of wind snagging its surface, the waters were calm. Below his feet, they lapped against the statue's side.

He imagined the city beneath him, with all those whose loss was beyond remedy. Those he loved and cared about. And those he did not: the great mass of humanity wedded to a life he hated, fools and Helpers. He felt an unreasoning guilt, as if through his longing for the vanished sea, he had wished this doom upon them.

A gabbling intruded. To the north Lyle saw a line of dark birds winding toward him, the green in their wings catching the sun. On the water behind them—

Was it possible?

A small craft was approaching—one made buoyant by air—an inflatable with a hull of silver tubes. Lyle could hear the hum of its engine. In the stern, a seaman sat with his hand on the throttle.

The birds turned a circle around him. Their bodies were thin with long snaking necks. One sculled its wings and descended, settling on the patriarch's head. Its beak was hooked, eyes glaring. It avoided Lyle's gaze, twisting its neck half around while the others back-batted and alighted on the craft.

The seaman rose from a thwart. His frame was large, black beard and sea hat, with oilskins the color of nickel, jotted and stained, as weathered as his face. He backed off the throttle, gliding. The inflatable's bow bumped the statue's hip, and the man moved to secure a line to the bolt in the patriarch's groin.

Lyle eyed him, perplexed.

The man reached into his pocket and drew out a watch. As he opened the lid, there was a wink of light.

"A short passage," he said in a smoky voice. "Like the time you've been hanging here. No time at all."

He checked the watch, snapped the lid closed and returned it to his pocket. "Unclip yourself," the man said.

Lyle was hanging in his harness. His pants were bunched and his smock was torn.

"Quickly," he gestured. "Lower yourself down."

"Who are you?"

"Blednishev," the man said. His face was solemn, lined and scarred, with thick lips and a broad nose. "Please, Lyle. Do what I say."

A quirk of lighting gave the man two different eyes—one silver and alien, the other dark and kindly. Lyle drew comfort from the kind one. He grabbed the rope with one hand and dug his feet into the statue's front, taking weight off his harness. As he sprang the catch, the gabbling mounted.

"Picket birds," Blednishev answered his look. "Our escorts. They're here to protect you."

"From what?" Lyle wondered.

The seaman motioned.

24

Lyle slid down the rope, letting Blednishev guide his legs into the craft.

"Here," he pointed. "Stretch yourself out." The seaman handed Lyle a blanket. "Pull that over you. You're shivering."

Lyle collapsed on the floor of the inflatable, picket birds eyeing him from the gunnels.

Blednishev loosened the mooring, pushed off and opened the throttle. The birds lifted back into the air, and the sentinel rose from the patriarch's head. They formed a line, and the inflatable followed them, planing over the water.

"Luck is with you," the seaman said without turning. "You're in our care now."

"Where are we going?"

"North, where the sea meets the clouds." Blednishev expanded his chest, as if he imagined chill winds were beating against it. "The birds know the way."

3 Your Only Chance

G roggy?" Blednishev asked.

"Where am I?" Lyle raised himself slowly.

"Don't tip the boat."

Lyle remained on his hip, eyeing the man and the humming turbines behind him. There was a black leather satchel by his boot. As Lyle's eyes fell on it, Blednishev stooped and slid it beneath a thwart. He pulled his watch from his pocket and checked the time.

"How long was I out?"

"Less than an hour," Blednishev replied.

Lyle sat up, expecting floodwater to spread in every direction. But the vista had changed completely. They were motoring beside cliffs, and the rock was unlike any he'd seen. It was sheer and blue and mirror-smooth, and the water was too. It looked as if you could walk across it. The craft was moving at high speed, nose up, skimming the glassy surface.

Lyle draped his arm over the side. A moment's hesitation, wondering at the speed and polish, and then he plunged his hand in. The water shocked his senses. It was thick and silky. He felt its coolness and blueness streaming through his fingers, in his palm and wrist, climbing his arm. He'd never touched a substance so sinuous or seen hues so rich—

Ahead the passage narrowed and turned, the walls looped with coves. Trickles brightened and multiplied, dripping from arches, ringing in pools, echoing in grottoes. Blue cloisters, turquoise arcades—blue, all blue, as if the rock had drawn its color from the water.

Lyle's eyes widened, his lips parted and the cool air passed between them. The fear and uncertainty of his final act, and of the life that preceded it, dissolved. He lifted his hand from the cold liquid, watching the stripe undulate as the currents embraced it, feeling a calm he'd never felt. It was morning. On his right, the rayed sun appeared above the blue galleries like an amber pecten.

"The capsule," Lyle muttered. "Am I dead, or dying?"

"Was that what you wanted?" Blednishev gazed down the passage.

"No. I wanted to live in a different world."

The blue arcades vanished behind them and new ones appeared, perfectly reflected.

"Like this," Lyle said.

He stared at the shifting swells, imagining the cool caresses and silvery bubbles against his skin. "I want to go in." As he spoke, Lyle quivered, his impulse mixed with trepidation. What did he know of this foreign element?

Blednishev nodded. "There's a place up ahead."

The arches were opening, extending into channels on either side. Lyle peered down their winding courses.

"Where did the flood come from?"

"Our maker sent it," the seaman replied.

"Maker?"

Through the glassy water, the gripping roots of the arches were muscled and twisted like the limbs of giant amphibians.

"I serve a god unknown to you," Blednishev said. "He sent the water and the birds, and me along with them. To deliver you from a dying world."

"A god." Lyle laughed.

Blednishev met his gaze, solemn as the grave.

"God of what?"

"Everything here, in this heaven." The seaman faced forward.

"Heaven is a reward," Lyle said. "For good behavior."

Blednishev shook his head. "Heaven is the wellspring of beauty and freedom."

Faces beneath swells, the woman on the bedframe, the shock in her eyes— "It was terrible."

"Terrible?"

"The flood. He drowned everyone."

"Were there some worth saving?" Blednishev squinted at him.

"Not all of them were salt mites," Lyle replied.

"He wasn't thinking of them," the seaman said. "His concern was for you."

Lyle was bewildered. Lost in a dream, a half-life.

"Why?" he asked.

"Because of your gift. Because you yearned for the natal sea." Blednishev eyed the silky surface beyond the prow. "Your hardships saddened him. They touched me as well. Can one young man change a civilization? That's what preyed on me as I ran to fetch you. As I sat by the kicker, watching the reflection of sun and stars, seeing the sunken cities passing beneath me."

"Cities—"

"The Empire of Salt is under the sea."

"All of it?"

Blednishev peered down, as if he could see traces below. "The broken buildings were like ancient ruins, the relics of a forgotten race."

He turned his eyes on Lyle. "These were your people. It's right that you feel some responsibility for them. But— If they were as my master wished them to be, the waters would have welcomed them."

"I don't understand you," Lyle said.

"Hang on," Blednishev warned.

Lyle grasped a cleat, salt spicules stinging his palms, squealing beneath him as he shifted his thighs. The inflatable rounded a lapis point, shivering, throwing a thick plume behind them. The coves here were close, their blue hollows like bowls on edge or the gills of a sea creature viewed from inside. Straggles of mist drifted from the openings.

As the craft steadied, Lyle opened his blanket. His clothing was rumpled and dusted with salt, as it was on the steeple. He felt his hair. Still damp. He unfastened the harness and drew his legs through it. Blednishev lifted his hat by the visor and set it down. His hair was black and slicked straight back.

"How well do you know your god?" Lyle asked.

"I didn't exist when he fashioned this heaven." Blednishev nodded at the coves. "But I was with him on many conquests."

"Conquests?"

"There are other blue realms. Worlds he transformed. Heavens like this. The cosmos is full of them."

The cosmos, Lyle thought. The world of Salt was far behind him.

Like most of his generation, Lyle attended school till the age of sixteen. As a child, he had shown little interest in either studies or Pleasures, and as he matured he showed even less. He received instruction indifferently, without complaint. And he viewed and listened to the mandatory broadcasts without objection. But when it came to optional Pleasures provided online, he kept his selector off and his attitude was scornful. In this he was following a family tradition. During the days of the Second Liberation, his great-grandfather had been an obstructionist, and the ideas had been passed down to his mother, who believed that work was essential to self-worth.

31

She chose to barter her services as a seamstress to neighbors, rather than becoming a Helper.

As a lark, Lyle learned to climb during his last year in school. A friend invited him to the boulders in the salt hills outside of town, and Lyle discovered he had a talent for it. His limbs were strong and he liked using his hands. Boulders led to bluffs, and within a few months he was testing himself on steeper faces.

When schooling ended, his peers found their place in Salt society. A few were driven by desire or parental pressure to enlist as Helpers. One classmate became a medic. Others were accepted into the large Salt military. But most had no thirst to help. They became Citizens and joined the large work-free population with nothing but time on their hands. Lyle went with them, but instead of immersing himself in the Pleasures and Conveniences that accompanied Citizenship, his climbing turned into an obsession. He was an only child, uncomfortable in large groups, and as the forced mingling of the schoolroom was replaced by the isolation of the hills, he became increasingly solitary. For three years his climbing skill advanced. Then the Museum director contacted him.

She was short, talkative and determined. The Museum, she said, was going to collect fossils in Fossil Wells. It was critical to preserve them. She couldn't use Helpers, but HQ had given her permission to enlist Citizen volunteers. Lyle's passion for climbing had made him a frequent visitor to the gorge. Could he help retrieve specimens from its chambers? The woman stirred his interest, and he became a member of her team. New demands were made on his skills, which advanced with the discovery of hidden hollows. It was diving in the absence of water, a dissection of the skeleton of the ancient sea.

In addition to retrieving them, Lyle helped clean the creatures once they'd been removed from their beds. He enjoyed that. The dexterity that made him an able climber fed his enthusiasm for the tools. And removing material from around the fossils led to carving models of them out of hunks of raw salt. You wanted to have more than their dead remains. You wanted to envision their movements, to see them in the midst of life.

Most of the Museum was devoted to the story of the State and its leaders, but in the small Nature wing, the team displayed its findings to visitors. Along with the fossil remains, Lyle shared his carvings. He found a receptive audience with children. The idea of the ancient sea and those that lived in it enchanted many, and their fascination quickened his own.

The director loved what he was doing and had play groups arranged beside the exhibit. Children who lived near the Wells were curious, and gatherings occurred in the community as word spread. Lyle found that those who hadn't yet started their schooling, or were in the first year or two, were the most receptive.

"Have you turned your Pleasures off?" he would ask.

The children touched their necks and nodded.

"This creature," Lyle introduced the first, "lived in sheltered pockets." He drew a figurine from his backpack. "It used its belly and tail to wriggle across the sand, and when the currents were slack, it unfolded these wings and ventured from home. This one's a girl." He flew it past the children's faces. "Her flesh is as soft as the inside of your cheek."

Fingers reached out to touch the creature.

"She loves the water," Lyle said. "Imagine what it might be like to be one of her friends, flying beside her. You visit the same places that she does. Close your eyes— Go on now, close your eyes and imagine. You're flying right beside her. What do you see?"

Lyle's meditations in the chambers began as rests between specimen forays. Naps with dreams populated by creatures— those who had left a record of their passing, and those no one had ever seen. When Lyle returned from the Wells, he would carve the creatures he'd encountered in his fancies, and he shared these as well with the children, along with stories about them. To the excavators and the director this seemed harmless. They didn't understand what was happening. And neither did Lyle.

The work had taken him to the deepest level of the gorge. This particular recess was familiar only to him, and it was his steps that had worn a thin trail through it. The path skirted a crag, winding among bromide boulders, past a honeycomb of caves, their entrances fringed with stalactites. A diving breeze whistled through the needles. This was a submarine place, where currents once flowed. Beyond the caves, prehistoric eddies turned, wrapping and pooling in a deep lagoon. Lyle moved through the evaporates, knobs and white bollards, through brittle latticeworks, sea shrubs turned to petrified

34

thickets with their roots in chlorite—a cobbled surface that once floored the sea.

Beyond the shrubs was a labyrinth of chambers thick with fossils. The chamber contours, shells and sockets, wings and blades, were like interlocked bones—the frame of a giant that might awaken at any moment. Lyle entered the maze, traversing from chamber to chamber, following where currents had whirled, squeezing through portals where neighboring eddies had broken through. The gaps and windows grew narrow, the shells less broken, the white wings more tightly folded.

At the end of the path, the Skull appeared—a large chamber, nearly spherical, a white bubble at the maze's center. Lyle stooped and entered, rising with the horizontal strata around him. He eyed the pale bands, tracing his fingers over them. The sad story was remembered especially well here: the successive rule of dwindling tides deposed one after another, the vivid creatures drained of color and pressed together, locked in a pale matrix. The story of a vanished world, and how it passed as the great sea died.

Lyle sank to his knees.

As sleep curled him, the white bubble detached from its moorings. With its human passenger, the floating Skull turned and caught the currents, and bore Lyle into the realm of dreams.

He woke with sweat stinging his eyes and a briny tang on his lips. His return along the path and the ascent to the rim was somber, a recognition, an acceptance. The creatures of the ancient waters were blessed, and those that roamed the salt crust were not.

With his pack on his back, he trudged through the city, putting one foot ahead of the other. Plowing through dust, crunching through hardpan. The sky was cloudless. It was late afternoon, but the air was still blazing and the wind hissed around him, spicules stinging his face. Where a sea had been, there was only a desert inhabited by ghosts and mirages. Powdered figures passed without a greeting. They heard phantom voices, saw phantom images; they gestured and mouthed along, immersed in their Pleasures and mood medicines. They took nothing from the grim fossil record.

The Salt people didn't see what was coming.

Centuries before, technology had eliminated most of the jobs. The cost of goods and services plummeted, but without work no one could afford anything. That led to the First Liberation. With the armistice came the Dipole Order—Citizens and Helpers. Citizens received food, shelter, schools and doctors—gratis from the State. Making things and providing the services was turned over to Helpers, those who wanted to work. With their needs accounted for, the only question was: what would Citizens do with themselves?

It was the founder of the State of Salt, the man honored by the statue in Memorial Park, who led the First Liberation. And it was he who introduced the first Pleasures. By donning a removable device—a tuner—Citizens could receive online content produced by the State. The selection grew quickly to include an array of entertainments: puzzles, games, contests and shows; fables and fictions; forums, klatches, war watches and workouts.

The first tuner implants were introduced to monitor health problems. Then, with the invention of the crystal tuner and the changes brought on by the Second Liberation, a tuner was implanted in every newborn. This allowed preventive medical scans and seamless Pleasure access, as well as giving every Citizen a full-time connection to the State. As part of the Second Liberation, oversight by the Helpers using sophisticated monitoring analytics became mandatory. Intrinsic Communication, as it was called, opened a rift between the two classes. There were Helpers who viewed Citizens as Pleasure addicts and treated them with contempt. And there were Citizens who thought the Helpers had overstepped their bounds. To assuage discontent, Conveniences were introduced—a new range of State services. These included such things as cosmetic surgery, fashion patches for pants and smock, and cephalic depilation as an antidote to the heat.

Lyle passed the cluster of crusted bungalows where he was schooled. A group of children approached him, silent, eyes wandering, lost in their tuners. The path descended into a gully thick with shacks, white hovels crowded among the gulfside benches. Around a bend there were more, with rickety forms moving inside them. Defeated, condemned to their Pleasures, limbs stiff, faces scabbed with salt blisters, their absent expressions framed in the blasted windows.

He approached a slumping shanty. The air was cut with heat waves and the striae seemed to undermine the dwelling. Lyle stopped before the door, bowed his head and stooped to enter.

Like most of his peers, he lived with his parents. Lyle's father—a smiling, well-meaning man with white hair—was ten feet away, seated at a table, tuning a Pleasure for fantasy profit, sorting play bills brittle as crackers. His mother, Pleasureless as always, set down the curtains she was sewing and rose to greet him. With a reassured sigh, she embraced him and spoke his name.

Lyle kissed her parched cheek. She knew.

She knew the depth of his hatred for the life Salt had tendered them. For the inhuman crumbling of body and mind. The mineral of the State was dispersing through all of them, solidifying their soft parts. Their internal chemistry was hardening to each other and to themselves. The end was in sight—the day, the hour their stiffened limbs and vacant brains would be locked into the strata.

"We've arrived," Blednishev announced.

Ahead the passage kinked and ended. Through the sunlit space mid-channel, a giant arch swept, blue and gleaming, its tapering legs rising and diving back into the mirror. The picket birds were perched on the arch, waiting. Behind them, a blue cove was wrapped, its naked rock patterned with scalloped fractures and branching veins. Seeps pulsed down, making the cove walls squirm like living tissue.

As the inflatable motored beneath the blue span, the picket birds straightened their necks and lifted off. They lined themselves out and swung to port, crossing a hedge of surf, guiding the craft into the protected place.

"Hold on." Blednishev revved the turbines.

He powered through the breakers, bucking and tipping into the cove. Its blue walls muted the surge, and in the calm at its center the picket birds were circling.

"There," the seaman nodded.

The birds' pattern was tight. They were turning over a sandbar the size of a small bed, waving their wings and purring excitedly.

Blednishev cut the motor. The inflatable's nose ran up onto the sand. He started forward, reached for the anchor and lost his footing. Lyle clutched him, saving him from a fall, grabbed the hook and leaped onto the bar, securing the craft before it could slip down the bank. The picket birds settled on the silver tubes, their webbed claws gripping the rubber.

Blednishev nodded his thanks, lowered himself onto a thwart and reached for the leather satchel beneath it.

All planned in advance, Lyle thought. The picket birds were staring at him with copper eyes.

"You wanted to change things," the seaman said. "To make Salt a home again for the sea and its creatures. But your efforts," he opened the satchel, "were bootless."

"You know?"

"I know. Your sculptures didn't prick them. Defacing the statue wasn't going to do it and neither were your mates— what was the name? Solution."

"It doesn't matter now, does it."

Blednishev dipped his hand into the satchel, and when he raised it something glinted between his fingers. He held the object before Lyle's eyes.

It was an ampule filled with sapphire fluid.

"You recognize this," the seaman said.

Lyle was startled, confused.

"My master was the source," Blednishev said. "The man you received it from was none the wiser."

"Your master?"

Blednishev nodded. "You were going to die on that monument. He saved you."

Lyle gazed at the seaman, the blue arch, the seeping walls of the cove.

"There's suspicion in your eyes," the seaman said.

Doubt. Distrust. Foreboding. What were the rules of this delusion?

Blednishev fished in the satchel. "I'm to offer you another dose," he straightened with a hypodermic syringe in his hand. "One much stronger."

"What is it?"

"A glandular secretion," the seaman replied.

"Powerful stuff."

"It couldn't be more powerful without being fatal."

"You're trying to frighten me."

"I'm trying to brace you," Blednishev said, "for the face to face."

"Why should I do this?"

"He cares for you. That's why he saved you."

Saved you, saved you. The steeple, the State— Lyle looked down. His shoes were still crusted with salt, his arms and legs powdered with it.

"And—" The seaman took a breath.

"And?"

"Your future depends on it."

As one, the picket birds bent their necks, bills pointing straight down.

Blednishev eyed the currents rounding the sandbar. "He's down there, Lyle. Our god, and yours."

Lyle stared at the coruscating ripples. The attention of the water seemed turned on him. There was an urgency in its whisper, a cold sorrow in the motionless air.

"This is your chance," the man in oilskins said. "Your only one."

Lyle looked at the hypodermic. "What do I do?"

Blednishev stepped over the gunnel tube, onto the sand. "Here," he motioned and knelt.

A chill breeze struck Lyle. He'd never felt so alone. Nothing remained of the world he knew, and the terms of his dream were closing in.

"Lyle—"

Blednishev's voice was soft and kindly.

"It's your element," the seaman said.

Lyle gazed at the water, letting the words settle inside him. Then he stepped over the gunnel tube.

As he knelt, Blednishev raised the ampule and inserted the needle. Sapphire fluid filled the barrel. It seemed poorly mixed, laced with jots and swirls.

The picket birds rose, muttering and treadling.

"On your back," Blednishev said, helping him turn, easing his shoulders down.

Lyle shivered, seeing the sky and the birds in midair, hooked bills twitching, their wings iridescent in the oblique light. He offered the seaman his arm.

"Take a breath," Blednishev said. "It will happen quickly."

Lyle felt the seaman grip his bicep. The picket birds descended, positioning themselves around the perimeter of the bar. The sand grains shifted beneath him, speaking in hushed tones, secretive, confiding. As the needle bit, the birds raised their wings, tips touching.

"He's in your bloodstream," Blednishev said. "Heaven is boundless, and the sea is beneath you." He spoke the last like a prayer.

4 The Power to Change

The sandbar lost its mooring. It tipped beneath Lyle. He turned onto his hip, weighting the sinking side, and the soft bed let go of him, slipping him into the water. The cold invaded him quickly, thrumming his muscles, ringing his bones. He shook like an infant entering a new world, weak, trembling. *My element*, he thought, fighting his qualms, imagining this was the triumph he'd dreamt of. The blistering heat would never waste him again. Currents circled his limbs, massaged his trunk, loosening and stretching him.

A dream, a dream, and this part he knew well. He was received by the blue, taken in gladly except for his clothes. His smock constrained him, his shoes and pants. He struggled out of them, trying to calm himself, letting the cold stream pass between his lips, hoping he could breathe, naturally, effortlessly. And he could. Water filled his lungs, thrilling and cold.

Bubbles trailed from his lips, a sigh trapped in the largest, wobbling as it lifted.

How deep was he? Six feet, ten, twenty— Through the submarine haze, the walls of the cove were visible, and when he turned toward its mouth, he could see far into its depths. Where the flanks of blue cliffs disappeared in the darkness, lights winked and rippled. The glitter of life. Creatures swarmed there, bright and busy, villages, cities— His senses strained, his sympathies charged.

Directly above the luminous scene, a silhouette emerged from the darkness like a brooding protector. A tall figure, a man in a flowing robe, looming through the backscatter. The robe trailed behind, a fabric of currents ribboned and braided in a myriad blue and green hues.

Lyle heard someone speaking, faintly. A fluid voice, shifting and changeable, deep and distant as the ancient sea, then whispering close, intimate as a childhood friend.

"Vapor and flow, vapor and flow. Bubbling silver and silvery blue. Pulsing with breath and laced with speech. Vapor and flow, the air and the sea."

The figure resolved, bright streaks flashing through him— emerald, indigo, aquamarine. Not a man, no—nothing like one. Where a head might have been, there was a swollen bell. And what looked like a robe was a curtain of arms trailing to either side. Their tips coiled as Lyle watched. The figure drew closer, fluid, cautious. A crosscurrent furled his arms. Below the bell, Lyle could see a hub, the silver-blue center where the arms thickened and came together.

44

"Water tells all," the deep voice said. "Every shift of mind and emotion."

He senses my alarm, Lyle thought.

"Water preserves, water secures. Water advances. Against its power nothing can stand. No man or nation—"

He wasn't swimming. The currents carried him. He was close enough now for Lyle to make out his features. There were eyes—silvery pools with pinpoint centers. Creases below, and a pillowy brow raised above.

"Submarine rivers," the figure said. "Sinews and snakes, fluid and changeable." He raised his blue arms and the current spread them. "This is my sea. I am—the Polyp."

"The flood—"

"I sent the flood."

"You saved me," Lyle said, "and drowned everyone else."

"Is this grief I'm feeling?" the Polyp replied.

"My father and—"

"In time, you'll forgive me."

The Polyp was close now. He raised a strap-like arm and stretched it between them.

"Smooth that wince," the Polyp said.

The arm's tapered end touched Lyle's brow, tickling it like a feather.

Lyle recoiled.

"This heaven will be your home for a time. And I, your host and guardian. It will be no idyll. A challenge is before us. A test. Perhaps an ordeal. We must make a passage—a hurried one. And it must begin now."

A thicket of snakes rose around the Polyp and crossed the space between them.

"My touch will seem alien," the Polyp told him. "You may find me repellent. But that will pass. I'm not going to harm you. What I'm about to show you will answer your most ardent prayers."

Lyle saw the blue eels swarming toward him. One circled his wrist like a bracelet, one coiled around his calf. One waved in the water before him and settled on his shoulder. The Polyp's touch was silky and cold as the sea.

"Don't—"

The arms crawled over him, clasping his chest, binding his limbs.

"I'm a sculptor, Lyle. What you've done with salt, I do with life. My grip is gentle, my manipulations precise. I hold you the way you'd hold one of your carvings, feeling your muscles, your struts, your curves and cuts—"

One eel pinned Lyle's arm to his ribcage, one circled his ankle and flexed his leg. One crossed his shoulder and slid down his back. Another belted his waist. With his free hand Lyle grabbed it, feeling it tighten, compressing and thinning as if it had no fixed shape.

"Let go of me. Please."

"A bony frame stiffens you, and fear makes you stiffer," the Polyp said. "In my ductile arms, your jointed ones click. Calm yourself, Lyle. You know how much easier it is when you're working compliant material.

"Look here. Your chest is flat. There's brawn in your trunk—"

Lyle felt the Polyp compress his middle.

"—but there can be more. I squeeze with this arm, use these to bulge your deltoids and make your neck swell. Pull here and here, flaring your back from your ribs. You're top-heavy now, broad-shouldered—a bull of a man."

Lyle's mind reeled. The Polyp was recasting him, changing his shape and proportions.

"Cinches, below the thighs and above the elbows—your quads and biceps bulge. And a hoop beneath your pectorals to give them tone. Burly, you see?"

Lyle no longer recognized himself. He was larger, with a conformation exaggerated beyond what his frame could support. And without a hint of pain or discomfort. He could feel the Polyp's thongs loosening. Would his body return?

"Even as you marvel at this new physique, my straps shift and pull the flesh from beneath, pressing muscle to bone, trimming your limbs, making them frail. The cord around your waist rides higher, shrinking your middle, ripening the curve of your hips. The brawn leeches out of you."

Loops reattached above Lyle's thighs, winching to increase the tuck beneath his rump, forcing his quads to flatten. A thong beneath his chest cut in, forming breasts. A blue arm circled one, squeezing the cone, distending the nipple. The neck thong pulled at his temples and pushed his cheeks.

"An elegant brow, a fleshy mouth—"

Lyle felt a welling of foreign emotion. The Polyp was changing his gender.

"Alluring, sensitive," the god effused. "Startling, exciting. Do you have any regrets, Lyle? Any at all?

"I want you to see through my eyes. My arms are slick now, silvered and gleaming. That's how they're dressed when I'm playing with life, when my juices are flowing, when I'm wiring nerves and grafting limbs—

"We're going to leave humanity behind. You won't like this—"

The Polyp looped Lyle's ribcage round and round, bands sinking deeply, dividing his flanks into rows of teats. He bound Lyle's legs, stretched his feet—

"Fins, a tail. Push the nose to the side of your head, lift your eyes onto stalks— Violate the plan completely."

Lyle was terrified. From his constricted mouth, a muffled cry rose.

"When I'm done," the Polyp assured him, "I'll put you back as you were."

Tapered points dug at Lyle's center. The god was opening his trunk.

"An umbrella with innards trailing. Flesh on a rack, a quivering sack. You're as flaccid as the Polyp himself. And now—" The arms pulled, all of them at once. "No head, no body, no symmetry at all. A tweedling hive, a crawling bed. I've drawn you out of your bottled pride and made you widespread.

"The next remove—"

48

Next? Lyle was frozen with dread.

"Enough of the known, of seeds already sown—enough in-kind reactions. If you're a god, make something strange. Something to shock the senses and steal the breath, something the light has never seen—

Strange, something strange—

"Let yourself turn in the silver gyres that circle these pin-prick eyes. Give up this brittle body and soul, revert to the plasma of pure imagination. I'm going to play The Formation of Life from scratch."

No more, Lyle howled in his heart.

"Steady, gently, softer, softer—"

The Polyp had heard him.

"Quiet your fears," the blue-armed god said. "Hurry, my snakes. Find your way back along the pathway to man. This sea is a home for beauty. For harmony and free expression. And these arms— They're instruments of compassion. There now. They've returned you to your original shape."

Lyle was suspended, slack, limbs splayed. His head nodded in a gentle current. Before him, the Polyp drifted, blue reflexively. A wave of calm descended his spine.

"You've met your like, Lyle. I read your dreams right. They were dreams of a future for those wasted by Salt."

The Polyp's bell glittered. He was rising and Lyle rose with him.

"The future is made," the god said, "by the power to change."

49

Lyle gazed at his arms, his heaving chest. His body looked as blue as the Polyp's. A desert creature who'd drowned in the sea.

"Move your legs," the Polyp directed. "You can feel your pulse.

"My embrace had another purpose. I could hear the Salt bugs, still sending inside you. One in your thigh, one over your heart, and the bijou embedded at the base of your neck. The crystal tuner. It was like the scream of a missile to me.

"They're silent now. Crushed to sand."

The god was hovering, arms coiled beneath him. As Lyle watched, his shape blurred, his color faded.

"Your senses unfasten from this suspect reality, feeling toward another. My presence remains, fixed in your mind. We will be together again. Soon."

In a breath, the Polyp turned and jetted into the depths.

"Lyle. Lyle!"

It was Blednishev.

Lyle rose with a swell, a large glassy lens, and through it he sighted the seaman. The bearded face looked dire. Lyle reached out an arm. His naked limb was bloodless. The winnowing water seemed to rumple his chest.

His elbow touched the sandbar. His back was against it. The bar was turning like a revolving door. The freezing water slid from him as the sandy bed came around.

Creatures, strange creatures. The ancient sea was their home.

Lyle began carving figurines during the sixth month of fossil retrievals. Within a year, the carving had become an obsession. He devoted every spare hour to it, teaching himself, learning through trial and error how to achieve the appearance of life. He saw progress, rapid progress. He had the gift of dexterity and enjoyed taking pains. He had a reckoning eye and strength in his hands.

Fossil Wells became a sacred place, a place for visions. On occasions, he would take a chunk of salt along in his pack and carve in a chamber, but most of the carving was done in the hills outside of town. At the quarries he could find rock salt in whatever shape and size he liked.

He would wake before dawn, load his tools in his pack and thread his way through the quiet streets. Salt flats spread from the city's edge. He crossed them quickly. First light would find him in a quarry, and he was shaping a cube or carving a cliff face by the time the heat striae rose. As the temperature mounted, the maker's fever consumed him. He would sit tool held in three fingers and braced by the opposing thumb, he removed unwanted salt stroke by stroke, until the creature was free and it stirred in his hands.

Most quarries were active. All were large excavations with steep cliffs that reflected the sun at midday. In the chaos of tumbled salt, Lyle would find a pit or a gouge with an overhanging roof. He would huddle there, with the rumble and drone of Salt transports around him, working till the noise faded and darkness forced an end to his labors. Then, drained and exhausted, he would succumb to sleep. The Museum director valued his passion and forgave his absence. And his parents knew not to expect him. With a small store of food, he could work for days at a stretch. When the sculpting fever finally broke, he returned to the city covered with grit, knuckles raw, fingerprints gone.

In its third year, the Museum's retrieval program was completed. Lyle's visitations to the Wells continued. By then his voyages had become a ritual. In the chambers, he dreamt of the sea and its creatures, and when he returned, he carved what he recalled from those dreams.

He descended into the Wells with towels and jugs. Once a chamber was selected, he removed his clothing, dampened the towels and bound himself, head to foot. When the sun entered the chambers, they became ovens. The air inside reached baking heat. Lyle curled in his moist cocoon, and it was in this steaming and disordered state that the ancient sea took him and bore him away.

He could hear the rumbling of currents, feel the riffles and drubs, and then gradually the green and blue sinews resolved. Rivers of sea were swooping past. Swarms of creatures, darting and turning, catching the light, bobbing and sinking, vanishing from sight. Feathered and fronded, clenched and slack, sleek as cat claws or crawling like scrota. Spotted, striped, muted or charged, lit by a rib knit of glitters or a grenadine of sparks.

One would emerge from the teeming mirage and turn to face you. Your subject, your study—the germ of a carving, keen and quivering, eager to be born.

Lyle's visits to the Wells and quarries earned him a reputation. The chatter grew fat on his distracted manner, his proud insularity, and the dust and dishevelment that had become his look. He continued to hand over his figurines—to children or adults, anyone with an interest. During the years that followed the fossil project, his skill as a sculptor grew, and his talent was acknowledged along with his oddities. When an opportunist entered one of the carvings in a State competition, claiming it was his own, the submission was instantly discredited.

His repute would have consequences—ones that Lyle could never have foreseen.

5 Sweet Chemistry

*L*yle was shivering, curled on the floor of the humming inflatable, wrapped in a blanket. He was waking from a dream of the ancient sea— one he might have had inside the Skull. But this wasn't Salt.

He brushed the hair from his eyes.

Cliffs of a narrow channel rose on either side. Blue cliffs, two hundred feet high. Was it the Polyp's voice he heard at Fossil Wells? How long had this god been whispering in

He lifted his shoulders. The inflatable's bow was in the air, they were moving at high speed. Ahead the picket birds flew in line, guiding the craft. At a bend in the channel, the cliffs gave off more, gabbling and joining the file. Blednishev sat on the stern thwart, hand on the throttle, his gaze fixed on the course.

Beyond the bend, the walls were marbled and flushed, violet where they rose from the water, ultramarine higher up. Reefs ahead. The picket birds made an S-turn through them— giant blue wedges with tide-worn shelves and bushes of spray, blooming and shedding. In the lee of the largest, there was a ship at anchor—one from children's tales—a schooner with the sun above its mainmast. The woodwork was silvered, the hull was gray-green. Blednishev steered the inflatable toward it.

"Alfred," he shouted.

A lanky man kneeling in the schooner's stern looked up. As the inflatable bumped its waterline, Alfred tossed a coiled rope. His skin was copper, his hair straight and black. Two men of similar hue appeared beside him.

A gangway was lowered and Alfred descended, regarding Lyle through tinted glasses. He was in his twenties, wore a blue rain suit and swayed from side to side with each step.

"Gobo," Blednishev shouted, and a big man hurried down. Taller than Blednishev, older than Alfred, heavy and unshaven, hair bound behind. Blednishev stooped and grabbed Lyle's left arm and shoulder. Gobo did the same on the right. Alfred was about to take hold of Lyle's legs, when Lyle shook them loose and rose.

He was groggy, unsteady, but he made his way up the gangway, holding the blanket around him. The three men followed.

As Lyle crossed the quarterdeck, a wave of dizziness rocked him. He stumbled and reached for the rail. Blednishev bellowed and grabbed him while the picket birds descended en masse, alighting on stanchions and gunnels, squawking as if a calamity were at hand.

"Is something wrong?" the seaman asked, face close, peering into his eyes.

Lyle waved him away, signaling he was fine, and the blanket fell from his shoulders. Abruptly the commotion ceased. All was silence. All eyes present, men and birds, stared at his body.

It was covered with stripes. Arms, legs, his chest and midriff— Welts, red bands, dark and brighter, aligned and crossing.

Keetch, the shortest of the three natives, hump-nosed with his long hair in tangles, fell to his knees with a reverent expression. Gobo and Alfred followed his lead.

Lyle watched with disbelief. "What is this?" he muttered.

Blednishev retrieved the blanket. "Alright," he motioned, and the natives regained their feet. A bracelet on Keetch's wrist rattled, strung with nacreous scales.

The seaman returned the blanket to Lyle's shoulders and

"My clothes," Lyle said.

Blednishev shook his head, as if there was some wisdom Lyle had shown in discarding them. "You'll be aft," he said. "There, by the wheelhouse." Behind the mainmast was a cabin with an open-air helm. And to the others, "Show some urgency. Let the cables down," he ordered Alfred. "Gobo, hitch the inflatable. I'll check the hold. Keetch, raise the pick."

Alfred brought the hoisting boom around. Gobo descended the gangway to get the inflatable in position. When Lyle saw he was struggling, he tried to help. With a feeble assist, Gobo managed to muscle the craft into place and secure the cables. Once it was raised and set dripping on the cabin roof, the three of them lashed it down. Lyle could hear Blednishev below. Keetch was in the bows, winching the anchor chain out of the water.

Alfred stepped behind the wheel and put a hand on it. He slid his glasses down the bridge of his nose, glancing at Lyle, eyes framed by creases, blinking, unsure. Then the glasses slid back and the engine rattled to life.

"Dig in," Blednishev shouted, and the ship started down the channel. He seemed to be captain, the natives his crew.

Beyond the reefs, the channel expanded and the cliffs descended.

Where was the ship headed? The birds seemed to know. They had turned on their posts, bills all pointed in the same direction. If Lyle trusted their stares, he was bound for a chain of islands emerging from the sea like the curves of a serpent.

They'd been motoring for hours. The sun was high overhead. The islands Lyle had seen from a distance surrounded the schooner now—round-topped hills, velvet green. As the ship wound through them, the sky turned dark.

A storm in the offing. But the vista was cloudless, except for one leaden cumulus that blotted the sun. As Lyle watched, the air grew darker and darker. Dark as midnight. And when the lone cloud moved aside, the glowing disk was white.

Some kind of clamor nearby, on deck. Lyle faced the noise, but his eyes wouldn't focus. He rose beside the wheelhouse. Or rather Blednishev was lifting him with Gobo's help. Alfred had turned from the helm. Keetch stood on the roof of the cabin, facing the darkness and groaning, making claws at the moon. The picket birds shifted on their posts, thrashing their wings. The figures all jumped, like characters in a film missing frames. What was Blednishev saying? His words were garbled, his expression confused. He gestured at the sea, barking orders. Gobo obliged, but Alfred stood frozen, fear in his eyes.

The moon was full—a giant hole in the night—and through the hole a pale smoke was jetting. The smoke billowed and spread as it descended, shrouding the ship, settling on the sea. It was dusty and warm. To Lyle, it brought calm and a sense of relief. But the crew felt none of its magic. They acted as if the smoke was a threat. It was doing unexpected things

The chop around the ship had flattened, the currents were halting. As Lyle watched, flukes of water turned solid. So too the moisture on deck. Brittle glass coated the cabin and sleeved the masts. The birds were unable to move now, their webbed feet stuck to their posts.

Blednishev forced Alfred back to the wheel and motioned Keetch to the prow. With Keetch calling directions, Alfred tried to steer through the openings. Blednishev and Gobo used boat hooks to push the crusts from the hull.

Lyle watched dumbly, like a salt mite lost in his tuner, mind slowed to a crawl. Nothing around him seemed real. What was happening? The Polyp was god here. Was this his doing? The smoke from the moonhole came faster and thicker. Lyle could feel the heat on his face. The masts were creaking. The deck was splitting.

"Spider Legs," Gobo bellowed.

Lightning appeared on the horizon, and a moment later the crackle reached Lyle's ears. The crew showed a new urgency. It was as if they imagined the bolts knew of their presence, were searching, trying to find them.

Keetch cried out just before the bow struck. The ship halted, the engine gnashed and moaned.

"We're lodged," Alfred turned to the seaman.

The two watched Gobo flail with his boat hook as the crusts ground against the hull. All around them dried cakes were riding over the swells, heaving like the backs of giant reptiles, converging on the ship. In the distance, as far as Lyle's eyes could reach, the sea was rigid, motionless.

Cracks of lightning, sharper, louder. The Spider Legs approached, seeing their advantage. Keetch was climbing the mainmast. He shouted, pointing over their stern.

Blednishev swore and spun around, and so did Lyle.

The round-top hills were pulsing. As Lyle watched, they burst like bubbles one after another. Behind them, ranks of mirror cliffs glimmered in the distance. The smoke was smudging them, smearing them— And then they vanished. It was as if they had never been there.

This isn't happening, he thought. But the smoke was pulling his wires. His muscles were loose, his legs rubbery. He clenched his hands to get sensation back into them. And then—his feet disappeared. As he watched, the smoke erased them. His head and chest were still there, on the ship, but the rest of him was ghostly, slipping away.

Keetch flew down the mast. Lyle heard shouting, orders. Gobo loomed behind him, and the big man's arms circled his trunk. Then, as Lyle watched, his trunk atomized and Gobo's arms passed right through. Blednishev tore open the cabin door and disappeared down the companionway.

There was little left of Lyle. He was a head on shoulders, floating toward the foredeck. Smoke smothered the ship. Its outlines were barely visible. The Spider Legs struck, dazzling him, blotting out memory. Another jolt, and the idea of heaven shrank to nothing. All Lyle could see were the converging gunnels. As the prow appeared, Blednishev raced up beside him, arm cocked, the syringe's glass barrel lit by a flash.

The smoke seemed to thin. The Spider Legs struck again, and again weakly, and then they winked out.

The rhythm of the sea. When he was curled in a chamber, Lyle could hear it in his ears, feel it in his chest. Through these vivid dreams, his romance with the waters became a devotion. And because there were none around him who could fathom what he was doing, he grew increasingly estranged from the city and its people. But he had no special malice for the State until the earthmovers appeared at Fossil Wells.

He was cradled in the Skull, on a distant voyage. The chamber bucked and shrieked, hurling him out of the dream. When he retraced his path through the quaking maze to a spot where a broader view was possible, he could see the giant vehicles at work on the rim. As he watched, the chambered shells were cracked and upended. No one could hear him over the racket of the tractors, but once he started to ascend, a driver saw him. The demolition was suspended long enough to allow him to reach safety, but there was nothing he could do to persuade them to stop. And no answer was made to his outraged questions.

The obvious place to appeal, and the only accessible to him, was the office of the Museum director. Getting an audience with her was easy enough, but what she told him came as a shock. Yes, she knew about the work at the Wells. She was part of the planning team appointed when Networks first proposed the construction.

"They knew the gorge was important—historically, scientifically. They wanted our blessing. That's why we were retrieving our fossils," she said quietly. "So we'd have a record of what was there before the Wells were destroyed."

"You never told us," Lyle protested.

"I couldn't," she said. "The State decided to keep things

confidential until work began. They're building a new Transmission Center."

"In the gorge?"

"The beacons will be on the rim. Generators and maintenance will go below."

"Isn't there some other—"

"They say it's ideal," the director sighed. "The Pleasures require more bandwidth. I love the Wells, Lyle. We all do. Everyone who helped with the collecting will remember—"

"We have to do something," Lyle said.

"You have a special attachment to the place." The director eyed him as if he was a relic found in the dig—precious, but alien.

Lyle wavered, churning inside. "The water's still there. Its spirit, its currents and tides."

"You mean—"

"It's more than a memory," he said. "The sea is still spawning creatures. It's still alive."

"There's not a thing we—" The director stopped herself, then yielded to impulse, reaching toward him affectionately, straightening Lyle's unruly hair with her hand.

"I'm sorry," she said.

A choppy sea woke him. Lyle lay beside the cabin, wrapped in his blanket. The air was dim, the horizon bronzed with twilight.

He looked up. The moon was gone.

The schooner was winding through islets, round-topped hills floating crown behind crown. Their contours matched the undersides of the clouds, as if they'd parted company just moments before. Alfred was piloting.

As Lyle sat up, he heard boots on the deck. Gobo was stepping toward him. With a shout, the big man summoned Blednishev and Keetch from the bow.

Blednishev looked worn. "The drug brought me back," Lyle said uncertainly.

The seaman scowled. "I shouldn't have waited."

Lyle rose to his feet. "Waited?"

"He's afraid he'll give you too much," Gobo said.

Keetch parted the blanket and touched Lyle's stripes.

"What happened?" Lyle asked Gobo.

"The Moonhole Smoke."

"And Spider Legs," Keetch said ominously.

"They found us," Gobo lamented.

"What do they want?"

"They're our enemies," Blednishev explained.

Keetch lifted his chin. "Enemies of the Polyp."

"You said this was heaven."

The seaman looked pained.

"Will they come back?" Lyle wondered.

"The Polyp will stop them," Gobo said.

"He'll destroy them," Keetch whispered.

"He has a plan," the seaman nodded.

Keetch pinched Lyle's cheek. "Let them attack," he said with admiring eyes.

Gobo laughed. Blednishev smiled.

"I am thinking," Keetch murmured, "of how things were."

"How were they?" Lyle asked.

"Violent," Blednishev said.

"Exciting," Gobo nodded. "Nothing stood in our way." Then seeing Lyle's confusion, "This isn't his only heaven."

Lyle looked at Blednishev.

"There are hundreds," the seaman told him. "Some near, some far. All fought for, watered and changed by him."

"People of every description," Alfred spoke from the wheel.

"The days of Nawkoo," Keetch said.

Gobo bowed his head. Blednishev sighed.

A reverent silence followed.

The seaman motioned to Gobo and Keetch, and they disappeared down the companionway.

Lyle stepped beside Alfred, eyeing the sun. "We're headed north."

Alfred glanced to starboard, frowned and consulted the binnacle, tapping the glass with his finger. The gauges were corroded. Two were full of water.

"The four of you are close," Lyle said.

"We've shipped together before. Gobo's my cousin."

The wind had picked up. It hummed in the rigging. The bow drove through the waves, raising wings on either side.

"How much farther?"

Alfred didn't reply.

A picket bird stood on the roof of the cabin, webbed claws gripping the wood. The bird was silent, but a low purring came from others posted like statuettes around the ship's perimeter. Their beaks were all aimed in the same direction.

"Where are you taking me?" Lyle asked the bird.

It turned toward him, copper eye glaring, impenetrable. The beak looked weathered, carved from fossilized bone. The jowls trembled as if about to speak, then the neck feathers bristled and the bird faced forward.

"It'll be clear by morning," Alfred said. "I read the sky. It's a talent of mine."

"Whose ship is this?"

"She was a trawler in bygone days. The *Mithostra*. A humble craft, but she serves our purpose."

"Which is?"

Alfred smiled. "She'll be a ceremonial barque, if everything works out."

Blednishev emerged from the companionway with Keetch and Gobo behind him. Each held a wooden box. They set the containers down, and while the two crewmen lit the evening lanterns, Blednishev removed the top from the first.

"We visited your world," Alfred said. "Gobo and I and a few of our pals."

Lyle was surprised. "You're lucky the patrols—"

Alfred waved his hand. "They didn't pay any attention to ducks like us. We saw your carvings everywhere. And we heard about your visions."

"I dreamt of a sea like this—"

"And creatures like these," Blednishev said. He stood with a white object in his hands. It was one of Lyle's carvings.

Lyle was dumbstruck. Blednishev held it toward him.

"We brought a few back," Gobo smiled.

Keetch drew a wad from his pocket. "Klensiar putty."

"We're going to mount them on the ship," Gobo said.

"Nawkoo was a carver." Keetch's voice was solemn. "And a lover of the sea."

"Nawkoo?"

"The Polyp's favorite," Gobo said.

"He was born in a fallen land," Alfred explained, "but he was an artist and a dreamer."

"When the Polyp saw these," Blednishev gazed at the boxes, "he paid you a visit."

Beneath Lyle's blanket, a shiver climbed his back.

"He was there with you, in the caves," Alfred said. "You touched him."

"Touched him?"

"You clung to the boards. You crawled up the side of the hull. You found your way to the helm." Alfred pointed at a little creature wriggling on the dash. "Like this flagelli here."

"Legs." Keetch stared over Lyle's shoulder.

As Lyle turned to look, Spider Legs struck off their stern. The sky flashed and crackled, and the Legs trembled closer.

Blednishev pulled his watch from his pocket. "How close are we?"

"Almost there," Alfred said.

67

Flash. Flash. The deck quivered. Lyle eyed the seaman, seeking reassurance.

"Are you ready?" Blednishev gazed at the dark chop beyond the rail.

"He'll protect me? What about you, and the ship?"

A Leg reached, striking to starboard.

"Don't worry about us." The ship's timbers mumbled and creaked. Blednishev put his hand on Lyle's back. "Show your courage."

He was urging Lyle toward the rail. "Are we there?"

"Not quite," Alfred said.

The wind blew stiffly. Across the deck, the flames flickered in a half-dozen lamps. "You're going to inject me?"

Blednishev shook his head.

Lyle was shaking. He put his hands on the rail. Another bolt struck, and he felt the blockage, the wipe of memory. None of this was real—

A deafening crash. A Leg divided the sky. Blednishev stepped back, standing in his oilskins, boots spread, riding the swells. Keetch drew beside Lyle, searching the chop, hair tangling in the wind.

"Are we there?" Blednishev demanded.

"The seamount is right beneath us." Alfred cut the engine.

The bird perched on the cabin had a crook in its neck. Its bill pointed straight down.

"You pray, you cry," Keetch was face-close. "For the life lost to Salt. For pregnant clouds and swarming tides."

"I do," Lyle said, seeing the truth in Keetch's eyes. They were frightfully wide. Legs sprang to life in them.

"Take his blanket," the seaman barked.

Gobo released the clasp and pulled it from his shoulders.

Keetch helped Lyle over the rail. An ear-splitting jolt— Lyle saw the crankled reflection cross the water. Then he struck the cold surface and sank.

Darkness confounded him. Bubbles sprang from Lyle's mouth. He felt the wake of the ship passing over him. He was tumbling, sinking. Bubbles, bubbles— There were none left. He parted his lips and let the cold waters in.

Had the lightning ceased? His sense of reality returned.

Lyle flexed his legs, reached his arms and spread them— not to move through the water, but to feel its freedom. The fibers of the sea stretched and wove back around him, dark and thick. Slowing his strokes, slowing his tread. His limbs barely sculled, and then they were still.

The inertia of trance, the obscurity of dream.

"I'm here, stirring my arms. The phosphorescence sketches my outline in teal. Turn your gaze down."

Lyle saw the brawling shape at a distance below him, hovering with its snakes all trailing the same way.

"Your heart is uneasy. I can feel it through the water."

The Polyp drew closer, riding an upsurge.

"Enemies of heaven," he acknowledged the threat. "I can taste your fear."

But feel none yourself, Lyle thought.

"I'm a creator," the Polyp said, his bald crown glittering. "But I'll engage them— For you."

Lyle heard the ambivalence in his voice.

"On my own," the god said, "I have no cause to fight."

He sounded wistful, nostalgic. Not at all like one girded for battle.

"Am I close enough to measure?" the Polyp said. "Tonight I am small."

Surprisingly small. His bell was no larger than an infant's head. The longest of his arms wasn't half Lyle's height.

"Am I so changeable?" He read Lyle's mind. "Or was it your wonder that magnified me when we were first eye to eye?"

The god filled and emptied with the current. Lyle watched his bright outline expand and contract, the hypnotic essing of his fluent arms, the silver swirls around his pinprick eyes.

"I'm a soft creature, Lyle. Supple as thought."

The Polyp sighed and pulsed closer.

"A mind with reach and breath. That's all."

Blue sparks sprinkled from his waving tapers, and the coiling ones were glowing blue wheels.

"Alien, inhuman. *Turn away,* a voice says. But Lyle's not listening." The Polyp spoke gently, softly. "It's the sea you want, and I am its soul."

The Polyp was only three feet away. A blue arm ventured toward him.

"Ribbons and cords, rivers and streams—"

Lyle watched the arm flex, sinews stretching and swelling.

"Water has arms that ripple and weave. Arms with echoes, whirling and twisting—"

The tip was inches from Lyle's face. It began to wriggle.

"What you long for—" The Polyp's voice was rich with emotion.

My dream, Lyle thought.

"Your dream—to create life and tend it. This dream," the Polyp whispered, "is as real as you want it to be."

Lyle raised his hand. The wriggling tip touched his palm.

"Lord of the deep," the Polyp said, conferring the title. "I can give you the power. To feel what I feel, and see what I see."

"Lord of the deep," Lyle said.

The tip slid around Lyle's wrist. A second arm settled on his shoulder. "Shall we do this?"

Lyle gave his silent assent.

The Polyp drew closer. The soft body touched his chest. Lyle watched it climb his sternum—lobular, boneless, the webbing between appendages bunching against his neck.

"An unusual passage," the Polyp warned him. "A troubling one for a man."

"No more troubling than death."

The Polyp slid over his clavicle. A taper followed the curve of his jaw. Another took a path up his temple, over the ridge of his ear, the arc of his brow.

"I know what valor is, Lyle."

Jointless arms, silvery blues rippling through them.

"A moment of doubt," the Polyp said. "The arm on your forehead senses mistrust within. The one around your middle, an innate repulsion."

The god was motionless, waiting.

Lyle closed his eyes. "Go ahead."

A prehensile taper crept up his neck, another crossed his cheek. Elastic skin sleeved the god's limbs, disconnected from the muscle beneath.

"To reach our destination," the Polyp said, "a bridge must be crossed.

"Your mouth, Lyle. The rise of your upper lip, the roll of the lower— I lift an arm from your shoulder and set its tip where they meet. It's sliding through now, touching the enameled squares of your teeth."

Lyle's neck locked. Fear bloomed in his chest.

The Polyp froze.

Stop, Lyle thought.

"I've stopped," the Polyp said.

What are you going to do?

The answer came softly. "Join your thoughts with mine."

I'm frightened.

"It will happen quickly. And then—things you've never felt or seen."

Lyle's head shook. He held tight to his fear, warding off panic, and forced his jaw open.

"A tongue and teeth. I can see your palate."

The current picked up, and the Polyp's snakes swept back, baring his underside. The arms' roots were red, and at the center—a pair of fiery labra.

"Menisci, Lyle. Glands filled with fluid."

The Polyp's bell deflated and slid beneath the eave of his bite. Lyle recoiled, sickened, desperate. The cold mass was gagging him. He could feel it pausing above the root of his tongue.

"The glands are secreting fluid," the Polyp told him, "sapphire in color. Not the infusion the seaman used, but the raw substance. It dissolves whatever it touches.

"A pinch of pain—here it comes—at the back of your throat. I've made a hole in the tissues and the brain's chalky case. A hole large enough to fit my eye through."

Could the Polyp hear his choked scream or sense his chest heaving?

"You'll remember this moment with joy, not dread."

The Polyp pushed through the hole. Lyle felt the tangled arms follow into his mouth, while the cold hub rose at the top of his neck.

"My front flattens to a membrane," the Polyp said, "riding up. Up the curving back of your skull, over the folded cortex."

Lyle opened his eyes. The Polyp was gone. He raised his hands and felt his mouth.

"I'm cresting your crown. Edging down, down—"

The cold presence stopped at his brow.

"Arms weaving through your temporals, bedding between gyri. And now—"

Booming, grating, drumfire quakes. Babbling in tongues, laughter, wailing.

"—they settle in."

Heart throbs, soul-sobs, scents of sorrel and clove. Clashing swords, creaking doors, explosions in violent hues.

"Following sulci, branching fissures, crisscross junctions—"

Peals of welcome, braying rage, a phantom limb, a toothless face. Then all at once—darkness, silence. Except for his pounding pulse. Lyle's heart was still beating.

He could feel the cold grip of the Polyp beneath his temples.

"My hub covers your forebrain, its arms in your seams. My front I let slip below your brow, sneaking my eyes behind your own, gazing at the mysteries of heaven through your lenses."

The voice Lyle heard was his own.

"Potent words, the speech of snakes, a kinship of tongues. My thoughts, your thoughts—our thoughts now, flexing their muscles. What a powerful place this is—the vase of your skull—with the two of us hashing inside it."

The water was turning around Lyle. A large school of creatures rose beneath him, flashing silver, each tiny dart lit from within.

"Strikers," the Polyp said.

More and more of them, like an eddy of mercury, a vortex so dense that no water was visible. All Lyle could see were the myriad slivers moving with a single mind.

"I'm turning up voltages, inducting, inducing— Not crudely now. With certainty, precisely. From inside."

As the Polyp promised, Lyle saw something he'd never seen: a thousand eyes, ten thousand tails flicking and passing, a million mirrors tilting and flashing. A great artist's work, sculpted from life.

"I can hear the synapses hissing and crackling. I can taste the sweet chemistry of our mated nerves."

Lyle's senses were mingling with the Polyp's. He felt something he never guessed he'd feel: access to the sea's ancient memory, unity with the sea's ancient pulse—

My idea of you—it was all real, Lyle thought.

He could feel the selfsame recognition in the quivering arms.

"Where is your fear?" the Polyp said. "There's delight in these channels. Wonder, magic."

Lyle felt a sudden power, hidden and private. Here he with the boundless blue all around him. If the god hooding his brain was the maker of life, if his arms fashioned creatures, if he'd filled heaven's streams— What did this mingling of the two of them mean?

"Lyle—"

The soft body shifted.

"Like men, gods have dreams," the Polyp said.

The surround of strikers was peeling free. A thousand silver arrows flew into the depths.

"Pointing the way," the Polyp said. "But not for us. Not tonight."

With that, the god slid from his throne, darted from Lyle's mouth, and disappeared in the darkness.

6   *Cold Currents*

wo months had passed since the first demolitions at
Fossil Wells. Lyle was prohibited from descending
into the gorge, but he flouted the authorities by prac-
ticing his meditations on the rim. The sight of him rocking and
mumbling, wrapped in wet towels beside the public walkway,
became part of daily life for the city. The planned destruction
of the Wells spurred Lyle's commitment to his dream and its
creatures, and his long days at the salt quarries continued. It

trail of white dust, sped along the road toward a niche where
Lyle was working.

He paused, hammer in one hand, chisel in the other. The
vehicle stopped, the driver's door opened and a man in a Salt
uniform stepped out. Lyle rose from the niche, holding his
tools like weapons, expecting the worst. His chest was slick
with sweat, his arms banded with muscle. The soldier was

larger and taller by a foot. He removed his hat and disarmed Lyle with a self-effacing smile.

His name was Jordan. He was attaché to the Minister of Culture, and he had come to invite Lyle to meet his boss. And to conduct him, if he was willing. The soldier had thin brows, soft lips and the eyes of a child. The Minister of Culture? Lyle doubted he had a choice. He donned his smock and loaded his backpack, and Jordan drove him to Helper HQ.

The complex was located on a promontory, surrounded by angular spires, overlooking the city. As the road wound through them, the spires flashed and quivered in the noonday heat. Inside the HQ, Jordan led Lyle up levels and along corridors until they reached an anteroom with a security pane at the entrance.

Jordan removed his bandanna. With apologies, he began to beat the grit out of Lyle's clothing. Lyle glared, and the dusting halted. The soldier was so eager to please, and so sheepish, Lyle grabbed the cloth from him and wiped his face.

When they'd passed through the security pane, a light went on beside an inner door. A moment later it opened, and the man who occupied the highest position in Salt Culture stood before them.

Minister Audrie introduced himself with a bemused flair, as if the trappings of officialdom were stage play. He wore a white suit with a white flower embroidered on the pocket. He put his arm around Lyle's shoulders and turned him toward a table beside his desk. On it were three of Lyle's figurines carved out of salt.

"I'm an admirer," the Minister said. On either side of his high forehead, hair rippled back, gray and black.

Lyle was conscious of the man's size. The Minister seemed to loom over him. His chin was broad and his cheeks looked hard. Jordan had posted himself beside the door.

"Have I done something wrong?"

"Not that I know of," the Minister laughed.

"Why—"

"You're something special," the Minister said.

Lyle eyed the cameras in the ceiling. "Am I being filmed?"

"It's nothing to worry about," the Minister waved his concern away. "I'm captivated by your work. Your sculptures. I like them very much."

Lyle waited.

"That's all," the Minister assured him. "That's why you're here. No other reason. I wanted to meet the artist who made these."

"Pardon me," Lyle said. He glanced at Jordan. "That's kind of you."

Minister Audrie winked at the attaché, and Jordan de-

not what he expected, Lyle thought. Suspicious, lips chapped, face burnt by the sun.

The Minister motioned toward two chairs fronting the table that held Lyle's carvings. The two sat.

"You're a tyro, a new player," the Minister said. "Like myself."

Lyle didn't understand.

"I became head of Culture earlier this year," Audrie explained. "But my affairs don't concern you. To the point: I see something unique in your work. These sculptures— They're so lifelike. This one here, with its flying tendrils and mosaic eyes. Or that one— You've caught it with its combs flaring. I can see the muscles twitching beneath its flesh."

"Texture makes flesh come alive," Lyle said. "Look at your body. Every surface has a different quality."

"You're self-taught."

"Who would teach me?" Lyle replied.

"Who indeed. I feel a fierce tension in this one," the Minister pointed. "An urgency. It's facing some threat—a life-or-death crisis. The one beside him, he's carefree, bliss-ful. Experiencing one of those moments we wait for. Strange animals."

Lyle met Audrie's gaze.

"They're all aquatic," the Minister said.

"My creatures have the sea inside them. That's how they reached me."

"You're referring to your visions," Audrie's brow ticced. "These cocoonings I've heard of. Why the sea, do you suppose?"

"The sea is a free place. The creatures—those that I imag-ine—have a freedom we've lost. It was the sea that formed them, gave them spirit and shape."

"I might have guessed," the Minister said half to himself.

"You're destroying Fossil Wells."

Audrie looked surprised. "I'm not involved with that."

"Whose idea—"

"The decision was made by Networks," the Minister replied.

"It's our only connection to water. All we have left."

"We've got our moisture transducers, our pipes and reservoirs." Audrie's drollery was cut short by the offense in Lyle's eyes. "I know, I know—"

He gazed through the window. His office faced away from the city. Hordes of salt locusts could be seen rising from the flats, obscuring the foothills. "Our leaders led us into a desert," the Minister sighed. "This is the home of our Liberations. Water will always be a lost cause with us."

"The Pleasure programs," Lyle said. "You're responsible for those?"

The Minister nodded.

"They're mindless."

"A lot can be done to improve them. That's one of my goals."

"Why don't you put an end to that idiocy and leave the

Audrie smiled. "Not everyone has the creative impulse. Let's be fair. Give Salt credit. Our people are free—they don't have to work. Unfortunately many of us haven't figured out what to do with ourselves. As Minister of Culture, that's my challenge."

His candor was unexpected.

"Your sculptures have been a puzzle to me," he said. "I sense a provocation, a judgment that sets these odd fellows," he gestured at the figurines, "above mankind.

"'Misperception,' I thought. But no—I was right. The artist, in his way, is trying to speak to some higher value." The Minister edged forward in his chair. "Exposure to work like yours might wake people to a new understanding. Of the arts, of life. That might make a difference."

The Minister looked at Lyle's hands.

"You're a masterful sculptor. One of a kind," he said. "I want to help you."

Help me? Lyle thought. His time was his own and he had no lack of rock salt. What he needed, what he wanted, was a fresh lease on life for the gorge, his source of inspiration.

"I'm interested— What is your day like? Where do you carve? Do you live with your parents? Any brothers or sisters?"

"You have that information," Lyle said.

"Well, yes," Audrie laughed. "I do."

During the days that followed, Lyle met with the Minister three more times. Then a visit was scheduled to Lyle's home.

Audrie was accompanied by Jordan. They arrived after dinner. Lyle and his father cleared the table, returning the cubes and cakes cultured from yeasts and bacteria to their cupboards, while the Minister introduced himself to Lyle's mother. She was in failing health and remained seated. She was one of the few who knew Lyle's heart. The sea was a mystery to her, but she was proud of the skill he'd taught himself. She knew how upset he was about the Wells, and she worried. Perhaps the Minister sensed this.

Audrie asked if he could speak to Lyle's parents alone. Lyle stepped into the alcove where he slept. He could hear what was said. The Minister started by praising him. "He's a prodigy." And, "Sculpting died after the First Liberation. Somehow your son has brought it back to life."

"We didn't understand what this was about," his father confessed.

"He's very serious about his carving," his mother said.

"His approach is his own," the Minister observed. "The style is new and fresh."

"He has my hands," his mother explained. "My brother was a Helper, you know."

"Yes," Audrie replied. "A surgeon."

"Erla's a seamstress," his father said. "She sews for the neighbors."

"They're well-tailored, I'm sure," the Minister said.

"What is it you want to do with him?" his father asked.

"We don't have a bad life," his mother said.

"I can see that," the Minister assured her. "I want to support what he's doing, encourage his carving, give him a place to work—a real studio. Bring the right kind of attention to his creations."

"That sounds alright. More than alright. Doesn't it, Erla?"

She hesitated. "He has his own ideas," she said.

"Would there be some standing Lyle might get?" his father asked. "Some position?"

"Possibly. If that's what he wants," the Minister replied. "Shall we talk to him now?"

When Lyle rejoined them, Audrie made an announcement which surprised no one more than Lyle, and changed the course of events for them all.

"This is a test," the Minister said, "for myself, for Culture, for the State. We passed, I think. I've gotten agreement to create a Fossil Wells preserve." To Lyle, "Your friend at the Museum pitched in." And to his parents, "If your son joins forces with us, he can help define the preserve."

Lyle's mother smiled at the Minister and extended her arms to Lyle. He went to her, knelt and embraced her where she sat. He said nothing, but his mother's voice filled the room. "Thank you," she said.

When he rose, his father grasped his shoulder. The Minister and Jordan remained silent, respecting the moment. Jordan, who had posted himself at the door, met Lyle's glance with what seemed like a cheer.

"I don't want you to take this the wrong way," the Minister said, looking from Lyle to his father. "But I think I could do some things to help here." He settled on his mother. "I've had a medic look at your records. There are some treatment options I'd like to explore."

The Minister's villa was in the foothills, nestled in the dunes. The sun was muted there and at the right time of day, gusts could be felt. You could see them stirring the salt grains. It was the last place Lyle would have expected to find himself, but there was an outbuilding with a north-facing view, and the Minister had it turned into a workroom. Here Lyle fashioned his creatures.

Audrie made good on his offer to help Lyle's mother, and after a brief hospitalization her condition improved dramatically. Her spirits brightened, and Lyle's father was grateful. They were both proud of the recognition he was receiving. At the outset, he spent nights at home with them, but before long he saw the benefit of sculpting into the late hours and sleeping in the adjoining bedroom that was equipped for his use.

It was a joyful time. Audrie had blocks of rock salt hauled to his threshold, which brought an end to Lyle's days of hard labor in the quarries. The crude tools he had scavenged and forced to his purpose were replaced by precise ones, fashioned by metalworkers under his direction. And he no longer had to endure the blistering heat. He worked with a roof over his head and a row of coolers around him.

It was in the third month of this residency. While the Minister attended to Culture's business during the day, he would often visit before leaving for HQ, in the evening before dinner, or in the late hours. Lyle enjoyed the visits.

On this particular evening, Lyle was completing a miniature of a creature that had presented itself the week before. The Minister had obtained a special dispensation that allowed him to resume his descents into the Wells, and the animal had emerged out of a dream in the Skull, flaring its mane, waving diaphanous wings.

Lyle was using a small hooked tool, lips twitching as he conversed with himself. He heard the door latch click and steps crossing the room.

The Minister stopped a few feet away.

"The current's lifting him."

"It's carrying me with it," Lyle murmured without shifting his gaze.

Audrie understood. Lyle's idea of the creature brought with it the momentum of its element. The sea had invaded the world of salt—briefly, but long enough to carry his carving to completion.

Lyle looked up. Audrie was wearing shorts and a rumpled jersey.

"Almost ready to polish," Audrie said.

"Almost." Lyle set down the hooked tool and raised a straight one. "I'm going to stipple him here and here—just pinholes. And sand his sides."

"Soften the surface," the Minister nodded.

Lyle motioned and they circled, following the light as it washed over the figure.

"Until tonight, I thought his mind was on swimming," Audrie said. "But now, with the detail you've added— The creature is hearing or feeling something. Reacting to something the viewer can't see."

Lyle glanced at the Minister.

"It's a startled pause," Audrie said.

Lyle pulled his fingers.

"You know—" The Minister exhaled, as if he'd waited long enough. "I would love this piece to be larger. Much larger. I understand why the carvings were small when you had to mine the rock yourself. But there's no limit to the size of your roughs now. Why chop them up? Think about that."

Lyle nodded. "Can we talk about the Wells?" He picked up a blade and began to hone it on a whetstone.

"Of course."

"You know how grateful I am. For everything you've done."

"What's the matter?"

"The plans they're presenting in these meetings— Most of them protect only a portion of the Wells. And the portion is shrinking."

Audrie shook his head. "I'll speak to them."

"The tractors are back," Lyle said.

"Tractors?"

"They're tearing up the rim, as if nothing has changed."

ister to a private conference.

"This minute?" Audrie frowned.

"With the Chief of State," Jordan said.

"Ah, yes. Certainly. Of course. Will you join us for dinner?" he asked Lyle as he hurried off.

87

Like Jordan, who resided in an apartment behind the villa, Lyle often took his meals with the Minister and his family. The attaché was younger than Lyle by a couple of years. His parents were Helpers and he'd been encouraged to join their ranks. His first job had been as Audrie's valet. The Minister was good to the people around him.

"What did the Chief want?" his wife asked as the meal was served.

"Programs." Audrie glanced at Lyle. "There's always someone lobbying for this Pleasure or that."

"Why does he bother?" she said. "He knows to rely on your judgment."

The Minister waved the compliment away, but he enjoyed the pampering.

"He's the youngest Minister," she told Lyle. "Did you know? The favorite child, you might say. It's no secret—"

"Lyle's not interested in politics," Audrie laughed.

"He might like to know the power you have."

"He's more interested in the power of water." The Minister raised his glass in a toast, winked at Lyle and drank.

"Water, yes," his wife sipped and smiled. The young girls on either side of her did the same. "The Minister of Water and Electric—people said he would succeed the Chief. Before the favorite arrived."

Audrie said nothing, but the way he knived his cutlet, and the look he gave his wife, spoke of some intrigue. Lyle took it as a reminder. There were reasons enough to be cautious with Audrie.

"Corinne's my current headache," he sighed. "She wants approval on all 'crime' content. Imagine."

"What nerve," his wife said. "Do you know Doctor Wentt?"

Lyle nodded. "From her broadcasts."

"The Expiations have made her a celebrity," Audrie smirked, "haven't they."

His wife growled with aggravation.

"I like your new animal," one of the girls said. "Is it pretend?"

"I'm not sure," Lyle answered. "I saw it swimming in a dream of the sea, so it's real up here." He touched his spoon to his forehead. "I dream about water," the girl said.

"Me too," her sister joined in.

"We're made of water," Lyle said, holding up his glass and turning it in the light. "Like all living things. Water from beginning to end, body and soul. Not salt." He glanced at Audrie.

The Minister didn't react.

"Anyone who wants more, wiggle your toes," the wife said, prompting giggles from her girls.

After dinner, Lyle returned to the workroom. The Minis-

arms, speaking with enthusiasm about what they might tackle next.

Lyle halted with a troubled look.

"What is it?" Audrie asked.

"I left my pack at home. It has my climbing gear in it."

"We'll get a duplicate set," Audrie said. "We're getting used to you here."

Rocked by the swells, by a ship and a dream.

Lyle woke in an enclosed space, but he could hear the wind and the water. He was on a bunk. Its outside edge followed the curve of the schooner's hull. Above, the hatch was open and first light filtered into the companionway, pink and mauve.

"All pretty now," a voice muttered fondly. "Fresh and clean."

A clang and a sucking sound, then the voice called out. Gobo rose from the bilge, shirt soaked with brine, eyes wide. "You're up," he laughed. "He's up," he shouted.

Gobo leaned over Lyle and grabbed a dangling rope, and when he pulled it, a bell rang topside. Then he stooped beside the bunk, rubber pants hanging by one suspender, his broad face smiling like a child with a head full of secrets.

Blednishev descended the ladder, then Keetch. Alfred looked down from above.

"How do you feel?" the seaman asked.

"Fine." Lyle sat up, remembering the previous night.

Keetch was wearing a woven cape, as if prepared for some occasion. He drew his hand from beneath it, bracelet rattling, and lifted Lyle's blanket. The stripes from the first encounter with the Polyp hadn't faded. Keetch touched Lyle's chin, turning his face, eyeing his jaw.

"How did I get here?" Lyle asked.

"He delivered you back," Blednishev told him.

"Off our starboard," Gobo added.

"Floating," the seaman said. "Unconscious."

"I used the net to haul you in." Gobo patted Lyle's thigh.

Lyle scanned their faces, listening to the ship's bones creak, recalling the moment the Polyp settled on his brain. The eddy, the euphoria—

"I sense a shift in your mood," Blednishev said.

Gobo grabbed the bell rope and tugged it again with a heartfelt smile.

"You're in the captain's cabin," Alfred congratulated him.

Keetch held his hand out palm-up, as if he was offering something.

"Your sleep was undisturbed?" Blednishev reached for his watch. Then when Lyle nodded, "Alright, the party's over." He glanced at Alfred.

The helmsman responded with a duty-bound nod and returned to the wheel.

"She could steer herself," Gobo muttered.

"Back to the pumps," Blednishev ordered him.

The big man tucked his chin and hauled himself down.

Lyle looked at Keetch. "When will I see him again?"

Keetch shook his hands as if they were wet, then one reached out and pinched the skin below Lyle's eye.

"Soon," Blednishev answered. "Very soon."

"Where is he?" Lyle asked. "Right now."

Keetch's eyes flared. "With his freedom, in the deep. Or flying to some other heaven," his gaze arced, following the Polyp. "A blue star crossing the void, rivers combed back. Or—"

Keetch turned his cheek. "—inside Som Thoosy."

Lyle glanced at Blednishev.

"His sanctuary," the seaman explained.

Keetch knit his hands.

"The tribes revere her," Blednishev said. "She watches over them when the Polyp is gone. Som smiles on his work. And she nurses his wounds."

"He's lulled, he's restored," Keetch's eyes closed. "Asleep in her gill chamber. Dreaming of shadows. Giving them shape. Dreaming of creatures his arms might paint. He rises in the dark like a wheel with spokes, feeling for places, reaching his snakes." Keetch stretched his arms in either direction.

"And for me?" Lyle asked. "What is next?"

The thin lips straightened across Keetch's teeth. "A necklet of holes."

In the quiet, the sound of the bilge pump reached them.

When Lyle glanced at Blednishev, the seaman turned away.

Keetch extended his tongue, as if he meant to touch Lyle with it.

Lyle's time at the Minister's villa brought changes. Many came quickly. Despite suspicions about Audrie's motives, Lyle embraced his suggestion. He abandoned his figurines and put his effort into pieces that were larger than life. His visits to the Wells were frequent and his meditations increasingly intense.

As the size of his creations grew, so too did the drama of his encounters. While his use of the Wells was officially sanctioned, the features of the preserve were whittled away. And while the demolition moved at a crawl, there seemed to be no way to stop it.

The relationship between Lyle and his patron matured. Audrie's enthusiasm for the young sculptor's work continued to grow. Despite the rewards of his office, the Minister seemed to enjoy nothing more than his time in the workroom. Lyle's disenchantment with Salt was reaching a critical level, but his rapport with the Minister couldn't have been stronger.

Although his visits were frequent, the gap between Lyle and his parents grew. His father was baffled by his residency at the villa. What was he doing that was so important to the State? Some of this was envy. He'd been accepted into the Helper ranks before his marriage, and then asked to leave when the discipline proved too rigorous. As for his mother, her faith was unshakeable, but it was blind. She kept a light burning for his future, without understanding the passion that ruled him.

Lyle's first crime against the State occurred during his seventh month with the Minister. He had been in the Wells most of the day, wrapped in wet blankets, deep in a dream. In a moment everything was chaos—shaking, crashing and a deafening roar. Lyle uncurled to see the white chamber cracking around him. He scrambled through the shifting labyrinth as the fragile cells jittered and fell to pieces. When he reached an overlook he realized what was happening. The demolition crew had set charges along the opposite rim and were detonating them. Lyle watched the tiered wells collapse while the crews on earthmovers parked at a distance whistled and shouted, enjoying the show. In a matter of minutes, the west wall of the gorge was a ruin.

He sat there until they finished, and was still seated when night fell. Silent, grieving, Lyle honored the gutted wall and the memory of the sea. In the late hours his vigil ended, and he climbed out of the gorge. As he reached the rim, he could see the line of tractors in the moonlight and rage overwhelmed him. He set off toward them without any thought of what he might do.

A watch was posted, but the patrol seemed at a safe distance. Lyle couldn't do any damage to the mechanics of a dozer, but he could do a lot to its electronics once he'd broken into the cab. He made good use of his climbing hardware, and the wrecking frenzy lasted twenty minutes, before a light appeared from nowhere and beamed in his face.

"You've got company," a low voice said.

The man's face looked monstrous. Lyle turned to flee, but there were others standing behind and beside him, all of them masked. Lyle raised a piton, ready to attack the first who approached.

A man laughed, then another.

"You've saved us some trouble," piped a woman at his side.

Red One stepped forward, lifted his mask and aimed his light at his own chin. "Doom to the State," the leader said.

They continued the depredations together. They had to

secret themselves twice to avoid patrols, but were quickly back at it. In addition to damaging most of the vehicles, they destroyed the temporary control tower. The team had explosives. After the charges were set and ignited, the group scattered. That was Lyle's introduction to the insurgents who called themselves "Solution."

The goal was a rugged cove, and Alfred had piloted the *Mithostra* up to its entrance. Keetch set anchor while Lyle and Gobo maneuvered the inflatable off the cabin and Blednishev ran the gurdy, lowering it to the chop. Lyle's figurines were pinned on rails and stanchions, masts and spars, and one was fixed to the prow.

Gobo climbed into the inflatable, then Lyle. Blednishev took his place in the stern, fired the turbines, and headed the craft into the cove. Lyle looked at the sky. The Moonhole Smoke had appeared just an hour before, but its jet failed to find the ship. The clouds above them were weighted with

glanced back, he saw a flash on the horizon.

"Legs," he shouted.

As Gobo turned, the crankled bolts appeared.

Blednishev clenched his jaw and revved the turbines.

The surges settled as they entered the bay. A smooth sheet with limbs shifting beneath. The inflatable flew forward, leaving a ropy trail in its wake. Ahead, a cirque of blue cliffs, with a dozen cascades like silver tassels shaking against them. The cove was filled with clashing, its waterline festooned with rainbows. Scarves of mist wandered the walls, and as Lyle watched, a great swirl was drawn into a cave, as if the rock had inhaled it.

A grotto. The picket birds circled its threshold, the clamor peppered with their gabbling. Blednishev throttled back the inflatable. Through the bay's narrow mouth, Lyle could see the *Mithostra* pivoting on its chain, riding the currents with Alfred and Keetch aboard. Behind it, the sky was flashing, Spider Legs advancing.

Gobo was beside him on the thwart, removing the blanket from his shoulders. A beam of sun lit Lyle's stripes. Then the shadow of the wall fell over him, and he felt the cold wind buffet his skin.

Blednishev killed the engine. Gobo grabbed a paddle. A half-dozen picket birds settled on the gunnels, and they were floating in.

The water was limpid, the grotto turquoise. Its roof was perforated and the crossing beams formed a lattice of light. Drizzles fringed the concave walls, and seeps descended them, dividing and rejoining, weaving inky nets.

A picket bird cried. Gobo pointed.

The lone guide was strafing the surface, doubling back and forth through the lattice, tracking something beneath.

"Ready?" Blednishev said.

Remembering the moment the Polyp entered his head, Lyle shuddered and nodded.

Gobo grasped the ring buoy and gazed at the water.

The picket bird had tightened his glide, marking the spot. Lyle stared at it, imagining the Polyp floating there, waiting. At the grotto's threshold, the flash of the approaching bolts brightened the sky.

"Now," he said.

Gobo handed him the ring buoy. Lyle slid over the tube and into the water, clinging to the float while his body absorbed the cold.

"Nawkoo is with you," Gobo said softly.

Lyle settled his mind and let go.

His shoulders sank. His neck, his head— The inflatable and its figures dimmed. A purring sound reached him. Was a current echoing in the grotto?

He turned a backward tuck into the depths. The sea filled his lungs. And then he was one with it—extending his limbs, motionless, watchful.

"I'm here. Between you and the grotto's rear wall."

Lyle saw the Polyp gliding through the rippling turquoise, arms half-coiled. Eyes—dimples in a pearling visage. Voice—

"I'm mastering your pulse, inducing it to slow."

Lyle watched the blue arms wind and unwind. The currents calmed him.

"I'm close enough now. Reach your hand toward me."

A network of creases shifted across the god's skirt. Lyle put his fingers on the muscular bell. The blue skin squirmed, reacting to his touch, and a silver tremor traveled up the god's arms. One snaked toward Lyle's face. He clasped it. Another circled his waist, flashing teal, chartreuse and eelrush-green—

"Courage, daring— The resilience of youth."

As the Polyp spoke, Lyle saw another snake uncoil, fining its tip. It approached, fingering the corner of his mouth.

Apprehension. Repulsion. Lyle fought his jitters and parted his lips.

In an instant, the Polyp turned midnight blue and darted between them. Lyle felt him pass through the aperture at the back of his throat. The chill rose up his nape, into the scoop of his skull.

"I'm in now," the low voice said.

In the water before Lyle, no trace of the god remained.

"Over the crown. Compressing myself beneath your vault, arms remembering their places, circling the gyri, sinking in fissures."

Again Lyle felt the thrill of contact.

"Pliant as jelly. Hub veiling your forebrain, eyes right behind yours."

Who are these enemies—the Smoke, the Spider Legs? Lyle asked straightaway. *Why is everything rushed?*

"No small answers will do. I must give you large ones. For some, the path of life is simple. For others, it's not. Great changes require great struggles."

"That's no answer," Lyle said.

"It's a preamble," the Polyp replied. "The invaders can be defeated. These arms have no match. They can be lethal, and there's no end to them."

The god's voice was measured, dispassionate. Not the voice of a conqueror.

"The reason you're here— It's time you know. But it can't be told. I must show you. We must go deeper.

"Headfirst, Lyle— Aim your crown down."

Lyle rolled forward and extended his arms. The sea parted before him. He stroked and kicked, descending at a steep angle, cleaving the cold.

"Exert yourself, make the strokes longer. Flex your back, let yourself go. Feel the freedom of the watery element."

Lyle felt a pressure on his brow.

"Kneading away these persistent suspicions. Good— Better, much better. You have an athlete's ardor, but— You never smile."

And you? Lyle thought.

"I'm not designed for smiles."

"Your voice is lifting my spirits," Lyle told him.

"Your well-being is everything," the Polyp replied.

"With you, I'm calm. I have a new confidence." Lyle felt the blue streams against his flesh, the sea's endless fluidity, its cool caress.

"The water loves you."

"This was my dream," Lyle said. "This. Just this."

Deeper he swam, deeper and deeper. Currents nudged him, stronger, more sinuous on either side.

"Here," the Polyp said.

The fronds of sea trees fluttered above, their rubbery stalks strung into the depths, like the flexing ribs of a concealed shaft.

"Down," the god directed him. "Down, down—"

The shaft was dim. Lyle finned and kicked, descending quickly.

The odor of sweat, a low laugh. A ricketweed sting, the sound of salt lizards darting through slivergrass. Moving lips, swiveling heads and faces, faces from Lyle's past, pulled like taffy, stretching, expanding—

"My arms flex in your crannies, stirring sense and memory. A breathless human, a boneless ancient—one interlaced mass, confused, expectant—

"Here in this shaft, this vertical lab, hidden, protected from the bloody remedies of man—

"Slow our descent. Slower, slower. Now stop."

Lyle twisted, lifting his trunk.

"There's a procedure we must complete," the Polyp told him. "A daunting one—but this is the last. Stifle your fear of me— Or let it pour out. Its extinction is near.

"I'm drawing an arm from a fissure, sliding it under my hub. I touch its point to my swollen menisci, wetting it with fluid."

"What are you doing?" Lyle said.

"So you may know what I know, sense what I sense," the Polyp replied. "The tip moves quickly, probing your lobes, spreading a fissure, dissolving tissue."

Lyle's ears popped, his eyesight flickered. "Stop—"

"Circling a gyrus, inserting again, cutting, dividing, dipping and burning, cutting and curling— Do you feel any pain?"

No pain, no pain. But I beg you— Stop, please stop—

"Brain, membrane, the meninges pierced—here and here, here and here—finding and parting and passing through. My other arms wait, poised in their grooves."

Lyle reached into his mouth—there was nothing to grab hold of. He put his hands to his temples. *Please, please!*

"The final step—fashioning holes. Points of egress in the chalky skull. Here and here, here and here— And now—"

Lyle clawed his ears with a silent scream.

"You are ready."

A sudden pressure built in Lyle's head, as if it was about to burst.

"I fill my center— And collapse it, sending the sea surging through the passages, bathing your brain, slicking the tissues, making them pliant. My arms come to life now, snaking toward the incisions, inserting themselves in the openings. No force is needed—I push and the tissues give way. My arms flex and twist, swerving and squeezing and sliding through."

Lyle felt spasms and stitches at the hinge of his jaw, circling his neck. And then the snakes were emerging, reaching out from him.

"You are the hub," the Polyp said.

As they stretched and uncoiled, the most miraculous feeling—like a fountain let loose inside him. Lyle was suddenly awake, suddenly alive, smelling and tasting for the very first time. From his nape and temples, from the corners of his jaw and the roots of his ears, curling and eeling in every direction—

"Snug in their sockets," the Polyp said. "You fit like a glove.

"The sculptor of salt used tools to carve his creatures. And now he has these."

Lyle watched the blue snakes ripple and weave, palpating the sea.

"They are the sires of heaven," the Polyp told him, "source of currents, the begetters of life. Does that stir you? Oh it does, it does—

"A god's work requires him to cut fine lines, to work in tight places. To carve while blind, shaping insides that must be felt, not seen. Using the most meticulous precision to insure the integrity of the piece.

"The sea tree stalks, the dim shaft— Aim your crown down. Dive, dive—"

Lyle rolled forward and extended his arms, kicking and stroking. The blue arms trailed back, twisting in the new-made holes, curling and rippling over his shoulders.

"Below—see it? There's a rocky ledge where the stalks are rooted. The ledge is riven with cracks—one large enough for us to pass through.

"Sleek our snakes and the gap will admit us. That's the way. Exactly."

May I—

"Go right ahead," the Polyp said.

Lyle tumbled and twisted, letting the arms wrap around him. *Free at last—* His neck wobbled, limbs fishtailed, his spine loosened and rubbered. *Free, free—* All the stiffness was finally dissolving.

"Heaven is a place to drown the senses, to rattle foundations. Lose yourself, Lyle. Be as lost as you like."

A moment later, he slowed and lifted his front.

"Do you see it?" the Polyp asked.

Twenty feet away, a pocket in the wall. A window box of life.

"Focus—use my lenses."

It was a garden, barely lit, in a sheltered corner of the sea. Hemmed with rock, shelved with sand. Covered with lush vegetation—strange textures, bright colors—their parts intermingled, crowded together.

"Quiet," the Polyp said, "not a breath—"

The lushness Lyle had dreamt of, the one his mind fashioned from fossils. Trepidation, and guilt—he didn't belong there.

"But you do," the Polyp assured him. "You do."

Lyle stroked and kicked, drawing nearer. They weren't plants, he realized. They were creatures.

"As we watch, they come alive.

"Ruffle fans waving, pleating and spreading. Crozier riddlebacks unfurling from the sand. Glass tunicates, red jellies.

er's blue arms. Crepitant finscribes, ovoid cloisonias, sponges that crawl. Anemones with trembling petals, cabbaged on the rock, elevated on stalks, or traveling in flocks with their pedestals fishtailing."

"You made these?" Lyle asked.

"They started with me," the Polyp replied. "But look at their selfhood, their fierce singularity— Closer, closer—watch them unpuzzle as I jiggle the focus. The finscribe skins shift, rephrasing their scrawlings. The cloisonias throb, their sectored hoods glittering like molten glass. They exist here, only here, in this sea.

"Can I touch them?"

"You can try," the Polyp said.

Lyle approached, swimming headfirst, blue arms rolling beneath and sweeping to the sides, the Polyp's creations before his eyes.

"A bed of mouthing pods, lilac-lipped, flaring to a shared beat. Among the pods, kisses and spotted cats, eyes on stalks and velvet rings, bird beak valves with ornate tongues quivering with the ebb and flow of the sea. Such curious beauty, such a thirst for life—"

Lyle heard the god's zeal. It wasn't misplaced.

"The magic lures you, the raw élan— These creatures know rapture. They're in harmony with the currents and each other."

Lyle reached his hand out. Instantly the velvet rings froze, the tongues shrank back, the pods sealed shut and sank into the sand. The life beneath him— There was a groove in the bed where his finger had passed.

"You could write your name in the sensitive shag. Worse than that—

"The garden is dying. The anemones are knobs, colorless lumps. The croziers are clenched, the ruffles lie flat, the cloisonias have drawn into their holes."

"They're fearful," Lyle said.

"It's your limbs that frighten them," the Polyp replied.

"Can't they see the snakes—"

"Predators can be mimics. But my children know my touch. Send your mind into these blue appendages."

Lyle gazed at the tangled mass, trying to feel them, to move them with his will.

"Focus on a pair. It will be easier if you close your eyes."

Lyle imagined two coiled tapers before him, unwinding at his bidding. They reached the garden's border and slipped into it, gliding among the cowering forms.

"That's it. That's right—

"There— The bed is sprouting. The pods push up, then the kisses and valves and periscope eyes. The anemones swell, the ruffles emerge and unpleat— All the creatures playing dead in their holes are returning to life. The garden blooms, and you float at its center with your snakes winding through it, feeling the lushness, the soft-bodied splendor."

Lyle opened his eyes, and it was as the Polyp described.

"They trust their god," the Polyp said softly. "He loves ——, cares for them.

"How did you give them life?" Lyle asked.

"Are you picturing yourself— Maker of heavens? Imagining a man with the arms of a Polyp, or the Polyp disguised as a man?"

"I'm a carver of salt," Lyle said dimly. "I toiled with chips and dust."

"You did your best for your creatures. You filled space with their emotion and purpose. I admire your talent," the god said. "That's why you're here."

Lyle was mute with joy.

"I want to teach you my craft," the Polyp told him.

A moment of disbelief, then Lyle's last defenses dissolved.

"Your thoughts mingle with mine, warm and human," the Polyp said.

"Cold currents fathered this heaven, antipodes for hells like the one you spurned. These arms live to shelter heaven's creatures, to be an unsparing god to them, and to know their hearts. And when the memory of brotherhood whispers, the romance of conquest calls. These arms dream of reaching farther—

"Dream with me, Lyle. Dream of a time when there are gardens like this everywhere."

The god's dream swept him away. For truly, it was his own.

A long silence, and then the Polyp spoke.

"Our interlude is over. Turn your gaze up. There—the crack in the ceiling. Swim toward it. Make your strokes count."

Lyle pulled with his arms, finding the current's bias and fitting his form to its streams, feeling a new unity with the heavenly sea.

"I shy from your brow, slip down the rear wall, draw my arms through your sleeves."

Lyle felt a cold mass drop onto the root of his tongue. He opened his jaws, and the Polyp streaked through them. A star in dark waters—the god tipped his hub, arms spoked wide.

Then the star winked out, and there was only a blue arrow shooting away.

Lyle watched him disappear. Then he continued up, through the shaft formed by the stalks of the sea trees, a disk of light visible above their shifting crowns.

He was rising quickly now, but something was wrong. Very wrong.

The day had fled. The sky was dark, and a full moon shone where the sun had been. Through the Moonhole a thick smoke was jetting.

Suddenly the sea around Lyle tore apart, and through the gap a nightmare charged: an enormous shark, a wedge-nosed machine gaping and screaming, with bandsaw gills and broken glass for teeth. It closed on Lyle's right wrist, and his hand came away. The ragged stump waved before him, painting circles like a signal flare.

Aerial bombs—picket birds diving. They plunged beside him, circling, wings waving like fins, hooked bills spitting air. Menacing, jabbing to ward off the attacker—

Flee, flee, Lyle thought.

With wild strokes he made for the surface, Blade and the Shark Saw right behind. Pain and a voice— His throbbing arm, a voice almost human. Behind, behind, right behind— A voice and words that made no sense, words like rocks that hardened in the mind.

Amid the pale scatter he saw Blednishev's silhouette. The seaman was in the water, swimming toward him with a weapon in his hand—a silver spear raised, taking aim—

"Lyle—" A glubbing cry, the murky shape close—

Panicked, Lyle swam toward the seaman, blood pulsing from his wrist, the Shark Saw roaring in his ears— The dark outline of the inflatable appeared above him, and then Blednishev struck. A hiss, a thin tunnel traced through the water and a silver shaft pierced Lyle's chest. Then Blednishev groaned as he pulled Lyle aside and the Shark Saw tore into his middle.

Lyle broke the thickening surface and grasped the ring buoy. Blednishev rose beside him, his wound pointed with moonlight, its interior shimmering. Gobo loomed over the inflatable's gunnel and removed the hypodermic syringe from Lyle's chest.

The Moonhole was no longer jetting, but thick scuds of smoke lay on the caked water. They were in the cove—Lyle could see the cascades hardened on the cliffs.

"Gobo," the seaman gasped. Beneath the eave of his glazed hair, there was calamity in his eyes.

As Lyle turned, a Spider Leg split the sky. It struck the cove's shoulder with a deafening crash. The air was trembling, and so was the clotted water. The *Mithostra* leaned beyond the cove's entrance, rammed by the chop, deck glittering, its prow spitting sparks. The jagged sea rasped, and a bolt struck the ship's bow, splintering the foremast. In the flash, Lyle saw Keetch stumble to the rail, waving his arms, his hair on fire.

Gobo grabbed him. He pulled Lyle out of the stew, into the craft.

7 On the Sea Stack

*L*yle returned to consciousness slowly. He could feel the rhythmic heave of the *Mithostra* beneath him. In his mind's eye the Shark Saw was frozen with its jaws open—a nightmare, loose in the Polyp's sea.

What kind of god would create an animal like that? Or was the Shark Saw another of heaven's enemies?

Blednishev saved him. Was the seaman alive?

Lyle opened his eyes, expecting pain, hoping it wouldn't be severe.

His right hand—

Not even an ache. And when he shifted the blanket, the hand was still there. Lyle clinched his fingers, making a fist, fearful amid his relief, remembering the shriek of nerves and the ribbon of blood trailing from the torn stump.

He was curled beside the wheelhouse. The ship was moving. The sea was clear. Above him, blue sky, and sun through the drifting clouds. The air was cold. Gobo's face appeared, hovering above him. The big man smiled, but his eyes were troubled.

Forward, a gabbling of picket birds and a series of splashes.

Lyle sat up. "How is Blednishev?" he asked, uncertain what to expect.

"I thought we'd lost him," Gobo replied. "I couldn't stop the bleeding."

"And Keetch?"

"Barbered on top."

Lyle eyed his right hand. "I'm just like I was."

"Wrong about that," Gobo pointed at his neck.

Lyle ran his fingers beneath his jaw, following the necklace of exit points left by the Polyp, feeling the rims and the moisture seeping from the berths. He probed one, and his finger sank to the knuckle.

The captain's bell rang. Lyle saw it swinging in the bracket, winking light. Someone on the bunk was pulling the rope.

Gobo straightened himself and turned.

Lyle rose, following the big man toward the companionway. Forward, the deck was scorched and wood had been piled to one side. Sections of the splintered foremast were visible in the pile. Alfred stood by the wheel, watching the picket bird on the roof.

Another pull on the bell rope—

"Coming," Gobo said. He started down the ladder. Lyle descended behind him.

Blednishev was lying on the bunk with the blankets pulled to his chin.

"We've slowed," he complained.

"Keetch can hear surf," Gobo explained. "He's in the bows with the birds." He glanced at Lyle, "Diving for depth."

Blednishev shivered. His wet clothes were hanging on a peg. Lyle's eye landed on the tear in his tunic where the Shark Saw had ravaged him. The seaman was about to vent his frustration on Gobo, but as Lyle knelt beside him, his mood softened.

Lyle cleared a shock of black hair from the pallid brow.

"What was it? What did this?"

The seaman said nothing.

"An evil spirit," Gobo replied.

"Did the Polyp create it?"

"What a thought," Gobo growled.

"If he's a god—" Lyle persisted.

Blednishev seemed not to hear. He drew a naked arm from beneath the blankets. In his hand was the silver pocket watch. The dial was flooded. He shook it and set it aside. "Let me see your hand."

Lyle raised it, extending his fingers. "You risked your life."

"As you did," the seaman said, "in the City of Salt. And for the same reason." He spoke to Lyle's right hand. "We are rushed because we're threatened. And these threats— Only you can put an end to them. Until then—" Blednishev met Lyle's gaze. "There are things from which no one can protect you."

Lyle was baffled.

"It will all be laid bare," Gobo said.

"When?" Lyle asked the big man. And then, with sinking spirits, to the seaman, "Why won't you tell me what's going on?"

"He won't allow it," Blednishev said.

"Because?"

"It would shatter you."

An odd sound echoed in the hold. Something was sloshing and dragging on the other side of the bulkhead. Blednishev seemed not to notice.

"I'll stay here," he told Gobo. "I'm too weak for the climb."

He closed his eyes. Gobo motioned to Lyle.

They ascended the companion ladder. As they reached the deck, there was a pounding. The blows vibrated the planks beneath Lyle's feet. Then it ceased.

Alfred turned from his piloting. "We're through the shallows," he said.

Forward, Lyle could see Keetch bent beside the woodpile. Around him, the picket birds lined the prow. As the ship advanced, a surface mist divided like cloth around a loose thread.

"Our condition is desperate," Alfred said gravely. "Our captain lies helpless. The responsibility has fallen on me."

Gobo wagged his head.

"It's going to rain," Alfred said. "String a canvas over the helm."

The big man ignored him, moving forward. Lyle followed. The pounding resumed.

"Does the Polyp speak to you?" Lyle asked.

Gobo nodded. "Through Blednishev. And Keetch."

Keetch was responsible for the racket. As they approached, Lyle saw he was swinging an axe, chopping wood out of the bulwarks, adding the pieces to the woodpile. Gobo seemed unsurprised.

Keetch stopped and lifted his head. He was nearly bald on one side. "She misses the deep," he said. Then a breeze lit up his features.

"A tailwind—" Gobo turned with a flying look, nostrils wide.

"The inflatable needs air," Keetch motioned Gobo toward the craft. "And—" He gripped Lyle's arm. "We must move Blednishev out of the cabin."

"Where will we put him?"

Keetch shook his head, as if that didn't concern him.

"You're destroying the ship," Lyle said.

His words jarred the native. After a moment, Keetch laughed, then Gobo joined in.

Ten minutes later, Blednishev was in the stern, wrapped of force raying from the prow. The carving pinned there had been blasted to fragments, but the others were intact. High above, the tops of peaks appeared like blue elbows, one behind the other. Lower down, where their wrists met the water, they were smeared with turquoise.

When Minister Audrie heard about the demolition of the west wall of Fossil Wells, his diplomatic poise dissolved. Lyle had never seen him so angry. It took the best efforts of his aides and his wife to calm him down. Aside from the irreparable destruction, Lyle could have been killed. An explanation came back: according to the demolition team's calculations the explosions wouldn't affect the east wall. Audrie was livid. Why wasn't he informed? Lyle wondered how much of his upset was on account of that.

After his first encounter with Solution, others were arranged. The group was youthful. In the privacy of their gatherings, some affected unusual dress and speech. There were as many women as men, and they took pride in flaunting their nudity and engaging in sexual behavior in view of each other.

Lyle was glad to find people who were hostile to the State, but he discovered there was little agreement among them. Some took umbrage at certain Helper programs, others objected to particular officials. Many, like Red One, wanted to replace the Dipole Order itself, but there were differing opinions about what form of rule would be best. A good number liked the idea of no government at all. Between the emotional tenor of their meetings and the romantic attachments, Solution seemed more about present passion than future change.

Lyle explained his personal mission to them—to open Salt minds to the miracle of water. "We are from the sea," he said, "created by and for it." This elicited puzzled looks and blank stares. While they were in harmony with his hatred of the

State, and while their leader saw him as an ally, Lyle came to be viewed by most as deranged. To his dismay, Lyle realized he was better understood by Audrie.

He was close enough to the Minister now to bare his feelings unreservedly.

They were together in Lyle's studio thirty days after the demolition. Jordan had retired. It was late, just the two of them.

"It's a terrible thing they're doing," Lyle spoke as he worked. "The Helpers you employ." He raised his file and regarded the Minister.

"They don't deserve credit," Audrie replied. "If a program's ratings are low, it's scrapped. If the people are pleased, they get more of the same. Their opinion counts for little."

"You're a sculptor too," Lyle said. "You're creating a nation of fools."

"I'm supposed to give Citizens what they want."

Lyle returned to his filing. "Have you spoken to Peavy?"

"No," Audrie said.

"He's a different man."

Convenience clinic. Certain State-provided Convenience procedures, like mood correction and sterilization, now seemed like evils to Lyle, despite the fact that they were voluntary.

"He'll never be anxious again," Lyle said, setting the file down.

The Minister watched him step around the creature's backside, using a sanding cloth. The piece was as large as a man.

"In the land of Salt," Lyle said with an air of whimsy, "people must be blind. It's the State's business to scratch their eyes." He knew full well the risk he was running.

The Minister stared at him. "I can't have you speaking to me that way." He turned on his heel and left the studio.

Lyle stood motionless. Would Audrie forget the transgression? Say nothing more about it? Or would he return with Jordan, or a full platoon, to escort him away? He picked up a tool with a curved blade and tried to resume his work. Ten minutes later, he heard the studio door open. Audrie was stepping toward him, holding a forefinger vertically over his lips.

He drew beside Lyle, raised a metal box between their necks and pressed a black button on its chassis. Then he sighed and nodded.

"You know what this is?" Audrie glanced at the box. "Dissidents call it a scrambler. They drive the gorillas in Security crazy. I've just jammed our tuners. We can talk freely."

The Minister set the scrambler down beside Lyle's sculpture. "I've been knocking heads with Food and Medicine." He waved his hand. "It's not something that concerns you. But the Chief's given me the nod. I'll have a say now in decisions that go far beyond Culture."

He put his arm around Lyle's shoulders. "I'm going to change things."

Lyle saw the fire in his eyes.

"We speak from the heart to each other," Audrie said. "I'm going to be the next Chief. And I'm taking you with me.

"You're upset about the Wells, and so am I. When I'm in charge, things like that won't happen. The people need inspiration—the spirit you've found in water. Salt needs a new soul."

Lyle peered at him. "That night— After they destroyed the west wall—"

Audrie listened.

Am I that trusting? Lyle wondered. *To share my crime with a Minister of Salt?*

"The sea was alive," he lamented. "It moved, it had thoughts. It gave birth to so many creatures. How could they kill it?"

Audrie sighed. "It might be best if you didn't go back there."

"We have to—"

"Now isn't the time to pick a fight with Networks," Audrie said.

"Without the Wells— There's nothing. No art, no desire. It's the sea's nature I'm expressing."

"Lyle—" Audrie gestured at the carving. From most

foreparts, viewed straight-on, suggested a struggle, and the Minister's eye was keen enough to catch it.

"This can't continue," he said.

"Their last days," Lyle eyed him grimly. "When the Wells are gone, it will be here—the history, the ruin brought to life." He nodded at the sculpture. "What they did as the sea bled away, how they writhed and crawled through the crystalline maze, seeking water— Until death overcame them and ended their torment."

"At some point, the grieving must stop. There are other subjects."

"Locusts and salt mites?"

"Why not people?" the Minister said.

"People." Lyle spoke the word with agitation.

"Maybe the destruction at the Wells is fortuitous." Audrie's manner was gentle, conciliatory. "Shouldn't art speak to our humanity? What can we know—really know—about realms not our own? Isn't it enough to find nobility and wisdom in ourselves?"

"The ghost of the ancient sea is watching," Lyle said. "It knows what we're doing."

"Have some compassion for *these* creatures," the Minister gestured at the invisible city. "Poor souls like Peavy, or the Helpers trying to make their programs better. Or Jordan, or your parents, or you and me. We're not creatures of the sea. We live here, in the desert. Don't curse us, don't abandon us. Use your art to inspire us, to hold a mirror up and show us our better side."

With that, he retrieved the scrambler and departed.

The Minister's arguments were hard to put by. During the days that followed, Lyle struggled with them. Audrie said nothing for a week, and then he returned to the subject. Empathy. Don't curse us. Speak to our virtues. Another week, another impassioned appeal. Then a sleepless night, and at the end of it, in the hours before dawn, the voice of humanity prevailed.

Lyle remained loyal to the sea and its offspring, but alongside them, he began working on his first human subjects. He did a statuette of his mother and a twice-size replica of her hand. A creature of the deep, followed by a bust of the Minister, which amused Audrie greatly. Then a sad rendering of his father and a portrait of Peavy before his operation.

For a time it seemed that Lyle had reached a détente with the State. He continued to visit the Wells, using chambers in the east wall for his meditations, while the demolition crews cleared out debris from the blasts. But one day, as he was about to descend, the demolition boss ordered him away; when Lyle refused to leave, he called for troops.

They were going to blast the remainder of the Wells, the boss said. Lyle's permission to enter was revoked. Henceforward, construction would be full steam. Generators and data banks for the new Transmission Center would be built in the gorge. A broadcast tower and beacon would be raised on the rim. Troops arrived and escorted Lyle away from the site.

As soon as they set him free, Lyle raced through the city and up the access road to Helper HQ. He arrived in a frenzy, sweating and breathless, shouting Audrie's name at everyone he encountered, demanding to see him. The receptionists and guards ignored him. He barged into the central hall, and when the attendants refused to skip him past the queues, he leaped onto the rotating island of salt blocks and made a spectacle of himself. Giant monitors filled the walls, playing popular Pleasures, and Lyle bellowed at the stunned observers, trying to reach them through the audio feeds delivered by their tuners.

Guards pulled him from the island. Lyle insisted on seeing the Minister, and his story was plausible enough that Jordan was summoned. After a hurried tuner discussion with his superior, the attaché led Lyle through the labyrinth.

"Something important?" Jordan nodded to him, fearful on his behalf.

The Minister was in conference. The two of them waited in an adjoining room.

"Go lightly," Jordan said. "They're meeting with the Chief in ten minutes."

A moment later Audrie appeared at the door, his back to Lyle, excusing himself. Before he turned, Lyle was already pressing him for action, explaining what had happened, why the situation was desperate.

As he spoke, Audrie's gaze narrowed. He seemed confused. Skeptical perhaps. He raised both hands, cutting Lyle short.

"This is very bad news," Audrie said.

Lyle saw the strain in his face.

"Networks is ignoring me." Audrie looked regretful. "Jordan says you made a stink out front. I wish you hadn't done that."

"There isn't time—"

"Maybe there's some final appeal I can make," Audrie said. "And maybe there isn't."

Lyle heard the resignation in his voice. "You knew."

Audrie scowled and shook his head.

"You've been lying to me," Lyle said.

"I had an idea this might be coming."

"An idea." Lyle's voice was weighted with contempt.

"Please—" Audrie faced Jordan. "I don't have time for this now." With that he turned and rejoined his meeting.

Lyle was escorted back through the labyrinth. His state was precarious, tipping from mindless rage to vacant defeat.

"I went to the Museum this weekend." Jordan spoke with a hush, like a child broaching a forbidden subject. "There were pictures of the Wells."

Lyle didn't hear a word he said.

They were striding through the central hall, and all the clamor was like the roar of machinery at a great distance, when Lyle happened to look up. What he saw turned him to stone. On one of the monitors was a live broadcast of the dem-

were blasted to smoke, feeling Jordan's hand on his shoulder. All at once his rage took control.

Lyle had arrived at the Wells with his pack on his back, and it was still there, loaded with climbing gear. As he raced toward the monitor, he swung the pack off, opened it and fished out his hammer. Then he was leaping across the desks as

121

Helper clerks dove for cover, boosting himself onto cabinets, and from there to the bezel that framed the terrible scene. Lyle hammered at the tractors, at the uniforms, at the exploding charges and the talking heads glossing the action, grappling the screen's backplate and spidering over it until the last panel was shattered and the show blinked off.

He came back to himself slowly. When he turned, he saw a hall filled with mute onlookers and shocked expressions.

It was an easy arrest. Ladders were brought in as the Citizens were led out. The guards reached Lyle quickly and he was taken into custody.

The chain rattled over the windlass as Alfred dropped anchor. Lyle grasped the gurdy, his eyes on the picket birds perched on spars and stanchions, standing sentry around the ship. They were restive, mumbling to each other while they pivoted and waved their wings. In the distance, sheets of rain angled toward the horizon. Overhead, the clouds were hammocked and low, heavy with water.

As Gobo and Keetch swung the boom out, Lyle lowered the inflatable onto the swells. The craft settled, and Gobo climbed in and started the turbines.

The *Mithostra* lay at a bend in the passage. The blue peaks wrapped around a towering sea stack, waves crashing against its pediment. To this stack their hurried journey had carried them—for what reason, no one would disclose. It looked to

Lyle like a bludgeon, burnished and ruddy lower down, blue and rounded on top.

Keetch waved Alfred toward the bulwarks and they descended to the inflatable. Lyle checked the clasp on his blanket and followed. As he stepped into the craft, he remembered the Shark Saw and imagined it plowing through the water toward him. Would the small craft provide any protection?

Blednishev raised himself from the stern of the schooner. His damp clothing was skewed and rumpled. He clutched his middle as if he was holding himself together.

"What's he doing?" Alfred muttered.

The seaman stepped to the rail with his satchel in his hand. Keetch waved him away, but Blednishev meant to hand it down.

Alfred reached, but the ship lurched and Blednishev bobbled it. The satchel fell and before Alfred could fish it out, it sank end over end and disappeared.

Blednishev met Lyle's gaze, glaring with self-reproach. Keetch yammered at Gobo. As the inflatable topped a swell, Gobo gunned the turbines and sent the craft heeling around with its nose toward the stack. The picket birds lifted from the *Mithostra*, winging ahead in a wavering line.

"Alfred—" Lyle grabbed the native's shoulder and pulled him onto the thwart beside him, scanning the water ahead of the craft. Keetch was in front. Gobo was in the rear, hand on the throttle.

The sea was heaving. A flurry of rain pelted the surface, then just as quickly it ceased. An ugly rip barred the way.

Gobo opened the throttle to power through it. The nose lifted, threatening to spill them, then the inflatable rocked down the far side. The waters here were whirling.

"Eddy dancers," Gobo pointed.

The sides of the green funnels were streaked with finned creatures, racing and whipping their tails. Funnels—twenty, fifty, a hundred feet across—moved with the current, tugging the inflatable from either side. Gobo zigzagged between them. Lyle imagined the Shark Saw following, about to tear through the inflatable's bottom. He checked the horizon for lightning. When would their enemies strike again?

As they approached the base of the stack, the eddies were crushed. The sea raised standing waves.

"Hold on," Gobo yelled.

The inflatable bucked, its rubber hull shrieking over the roar of the motors and the crashing of breakers.

Keetch cried out, gesturing with both arms.

Through the spindrift, Lyle saw the picket birds circle and sink, settling on a pile of boulders. The stack towered over them now, girdled by mists, blue where its head aimed at the clouds. Keetch was searching the summit—

"Watch out," Alfred warned.

The last of the standing waves collapsed, the inflatable seesawed and plunged, landing hard. Spray struck Lyle's face, buckshot from the breakers— Bursts of froth were hasping and curling back into the surge.

A skirt of seamed rock appeared, purplish, creased like the Polyp's web.

Gobo gunned the inflatable, swerving and broaching on the rock. Keetch slung a coiled line over his shoulder and sprang out, scrambling up the skirt, looking for a spot to secure the line. Gobo killed the engines.

Lyle climbed out and set his feet on the streaming shelf. On either side, breakers were bursting, sending tremors into his legs. Alfred hurried past him, sloshing through the shallows, onto the shore.

The tidal weeds were wattled, yellow-green, trimmed with golden beads. Among the fallen blue boulders, Lyle recognized the remains of creatures he'd seen in the Polyp's garden. Finscribes, heaped by tides. A million cast cartilages, hieroglyphs glittering like those on Keetch's bracelet, rattling in the wind as they did on his wrist.

The picket birds took wing, leading the way.

In an aisle between boulders, Alfred found an overgrown path. He turned, indicated the direction and started up. Lyle followed, then Keetch, with Gobo in the rear. They moved through jade-blue scrub, leaves plaited and dripping. Alfred parted the webbed branches, making tight switchbacks. "Watch your step," he warned at a drop-off.

For the first time since arriving in heaven, Lyle felt the earth firmly beneath him. It was unsettling. He missed the rocking, the rhythm of the swells. But he could still hear the rumble and crash. The power of the sea was all around him.

Alfred halted. He was fixed on something—

Lyle saw a dark face peering through the leaves.

It was a weatherworn carving. The damp on its bulging

eyes and lips made them glisten. Gobo used the pause to take the lead.

"Here the dead speak," Keetch said. "From the totems and the trees. In the fog-drip and the breeze."

The picket birds lined the trail, pinions fanning to shepherd them along, taking wing as they passed and alighting ahead.

"The tribes of the Polyp— They live together beneath the sea," Keetch said. "They thrive in his currents, the freedom he's given them. They make what they will of themselves. But they must not forget: they sprang from a dream of grace and harmony."

Lyle glanced back, seeing Keetch's dark eyes, his lopsided hair, the inscrutable smile.

"They're boneless," Lyle said, thinking of the creatures in the garden.

"They feed on the drifting blooms," Keetch went on, "filtering his sea. They weren't designed to take life from each other."

He spoke with the authority of the Polyp. And with the same shaded simplicity.

"Humans take lives," Lyle pointed out.

Keetch nodded meaningly. A long moment of silence, and then: "All the soft-bodied people thronging his seas feel the Polyp's care. They have fears, but not many. They know what distances his arms can reach."

Trees rose up, strange trees with banded trunks and fern fronds for boughs. The fronds had silver ribs and lapis barbules, and out of a nest at the top of each, croziers unfurled.

"In this far archipelago, the Polyp practiced his art. For ages he labored and dreamt, spawned and slept, never thinking of worlds beyond his own.

"What set the Polyp on his search for Nawkoo? An impulse or some long-hatched plan? Could he find no one among his own creations? Why did he seek him in a fallen land? The stories are lost.

"But those who cherish Nawkoo's memory—"

Lyle heard the pride in Keetch's voice.

"—know he was young—your age, Lyle—when their fates were mingled. The Polyp and Nawkoo. A bond like no other, this man and this god. Who can imagine the feelings they shared, the words, the thoughts, when their futures were joined on the back of Som Thoosy. A blessing for them and for heaven. And for all those lands who knew nothing of either.

"He was a carver, an artist. But joined to this passion, there was rage in Nawkoo, a renegade fire. He dreamt of conquest, of battles to turn barren places into fruitful seas, of a triumphant return to his hellish home. And because they were Nawkoo's dreams, the Polyp shared them.

When the pledge was made, the god gave up his quiet. Bid farewell to the humble life and his adoring Som. They journeyed to distant lands, fallen worlds with people wretched in spirit.

"They warred and conquered, drowning nations, putting all to the test. The creatures that pleased them, they bred and reshaped, making them supple, ready for the sea. Those that did not were cast away. All the families and clans in those far-flung heavens, the millions that dwell in those radiant cities— All honor the hour the Polyp was united with Nawkoo and trace their happiness back to then."

"Cast away?" Lyle said.

The tree ferns were taller, their tops blue fountains. The fronds swept over them, forming glittering arches. The picket birds lifted with *tworps* and *larps*, a liquid sound, like droplets released.

"Yes," Keetch replied. "Cast away. What Nawkoo judged unfit, he was not afraid to destroy. His vengeance against the land of his birth is legend. But the god calmed his rage. From the Polyp, Nawkoo learned judgment and mercy. 'Every world has children,' the Polyp tells us. 'And most who are grown still have a child inside.'"

Lyle saw the zeal of the mythmaker in Keetch's face.

"Expeditions—long. Setbacks—often. There are stories, many of them, telling of their triumphs. That is what the tribes want to hear. But for every victory there was a crushing defeat. Enslaved people siding with their leaders—tyrants and thieves. Lies, brainwashing— Our father, our god— They called him a monster, a freak.

"A triumph might be won, but at a terrible cost. It could take ages to sort the good from the bad. For Nawkoo, there was nothing worse than retreat. But for those fighting alongside them, there were casualties and wounds. And if the field was abandoned, their allies were doomed."

Gobo turned his head, brow rumpled, recalling.

"There were times," Keetch went on, "when conflicts brought the combat here, and our people paid the price. Through it all, Nawkoo was the soul of belief. The Polyp guided him, sometimes sternly, but he never denied him. Their campaigns brought change, and from the new realms, new generations sprang—lines that fulfilled the true promise of heaven.

"The Polyp remained with him to the end of his life."

The tree ferns were draped with stoles—the relict fronds, dried and helixed, of seasons past. The clouds above Lyle were livid, the billows looked bruised and swollen, about to burst.

"Some thought Nawkoo would live forever. But he was mortal, and his day finally came. After seventeen centuries of conflict and creation, he died in his homeland. Peacefully, witnesses agreed.

"It was in the middle of winter," Keetch said. "On the darkest day of the year. While the tribes grieved and prayed, the Polyp dragged himself from the dead man, ragged and incomplete. And when the ceremonies were over, he vanished.

"Moons came and went, and the people waited. Would the Polyp recover from Nawkoo's passing? He did, of course.

"After ten moons, he returned to his people. The appetite for conquest had left him. Picket birds were posted in the remade worlds, and they summoned him only when things were grave. The Polyp resumed his former ways. He found pleasure in the villages of his native sea and made children his life. And his nights he spent with Som Thoosy."

The path steepened. Weather had scoured the rock, leaving naked blue marble. Lyle chose his steps carefully. Ahead, the fern crowns had flattened, blue wheels turning as the wind twisted them. From the rims, water beads dashed in silver crescents.

Alfred lagged. He looked spooked.

As they approached the top of the stack, the tree ferns thinned and the view expanded. The picket birds lined the shelves of an outcrop to the left, its walls washed with lime. The odor was intense—a place of conceiving, of disgorging and feeding, of birth and voiding.

A dizzying place. Lyle gazed at the sweep of the bobbing peaks, feeling again the power of the sea. Far below, cauldrons churned, sucking and foaming.

"He was small," Keetch said, "like you and me. But there were times when the Polyp made him a giant. To fit him for battle." He pointed at a distant bay. "They'd see him through the mist in water to his waist, or striding past a cape with his legs in the current and his head in the clouds."

All the birds lifted at once, gabbling and beating their wings, drawing Lyle's attention to the right, where the pathway ended. Two carved posts—one still erect, the other collapsed. And beyond the posts, a small wooden hut with a solitary tree fern rooted beside it. The picket birds circled over the tree and settled on its spokes.

Gobo stopped. He reached his hand out with a private smile, then drew it back.

Keetch peered at the hut through narrowed eyes, as if he could hear it speaking. "We go no farther." He nodded at the path. "Only you."

Lyle shivered, suddenly fearful. *Only you.* What was waiting for him? How could he have arrived at this strange place, exposed and alone, without knowing why? Keetch stooped and then bowed to Lyle, lowering himself to his knees. Gobo did the same.

Lyle put his foot forward, watching the damp grass quiver. Slow steps with bare feet. Past Gobo and the standing post—

The hut was silvered with age, its front rotted away.

He pulled the blanket around him, naked beneath it, chilled to the bone. The aged enclosure stood in a pool of sorrow, a damp shadow fed by the fronds dripping above. Moss had made a green tongue of its floor. The picket birds watched his feet sink into it. He was crossing the threshold.

Inside, the hut was moldy and dank. The planks of its roof were warped, bars of sky visible between them. Lyle saw an oblong table against the rear wall. There was a large weathered box on it, the size of an infant's crib. As he drew closer, a carved face appeared in the wood, eyes bulging, mouth wide.

Fists were raised on either side, as if to ward off intruders.

Closer, closer—

Lyle put his hands on the lid. The wood was soft and damp.

The lid was loose.

He raised it, admitting the light.

There was a withered body inside. Naked, on its back, knees flexed. The leathery skin was banded with scarlet stripes. Across the sunken chest, its arms were folded. The left hand was curled, the right ended in a stump.

Its face was hidden by a shroud.

Lyle grasped the faded cloth, seeing symbols and scrawls. He peeled it back—

The corpse's eyes met his.

The soul of belief, Lyle thought. The eyes glimmered with life. They were stone, he realized—pearly blue, marbled with turquoise swirls. The hero's brow was mottled, his cheeks were hollow. The ropes of hair, braided and coiled with painstaking care, lay detached on his shoulders. And the holes beneath his jaw, around ear and temple, were withered and cracked.

A rustle of branches, the purr of picket birds— The sounds reached Lyle like echoes of the procession that had climbed the path, bearing the box.

The laurel of conquest, the glory that rayed from this head— All gone. There was nothing to see but the stony eyes, some silver daubs and a chaplet of beads.

Nawkoo. Brother of the Polyp. A grinning corpse.

Suddenly the planks beneath Lyle's feet were thrumming. A burning odor. At the corner of his vision, tendrils of steam or smoke.

A crash, and rumbling at a distance—

He backed away from the casket, swaying, shaking, vision

blurred. He clamped his lids, but the defect only grew worse. The image of Nawkoo was smeared, as if someone meant to rub it out. He lifted his hands to his eyes and sparks spit from his fingers. *Spider Legs*—

Screeching, gabbling—the picket birds rose, keen to the threat. Lyle turned, lurching over the moldy planks, stumbling out of the gravehouse.

The light that met him was blinding. The air was crushed. His head was rent.

Lyle's body rang like a steel pipe struck by a hammer. A strobe of afterimages—the crew did a spastic dance in dead silence, while picket birds thrashed their wings in his face. "Help," he whispered.

His hearing returned. The natives were shouting, grabbing, the frenzied birds mobbing to protect him. Craze marks rayed across his chest, as if the spider had fractured his frame. What was he doing here? Why was this happening? His thoughts came slowly now, one at time. He was on a sea stack. The stack was quaking. The clouds rumbled and roiled, and as Lyle looked up they parted. An enormous white bolt—a jointed Leg, glowing orange where it flexed—reached through and struck him.

His body convulsed and his mind shrank. Hateful light, thunder rolling—

Men with copper skin— Tugging, forcing him along. *Who are they? What do they want?* Lyle reached his arms out, feeling through the dazzle, his temple throbbing— Twisting tree ferns, a lime-splashed wall, birds screeching with wild eyes—

"Over, over," the short man shouted, stripping a blanket from his shoulders.

Lyle saw the sheer fall. They'd led him to the brink. The drop was straight into the sea. Above him, the clouds parted, the rumble mounted—

"Where are you?" he cried.

Far below, nets of foam pulled apart. Beneath a lens-shaped swell, the Polyp's shadow rose, bigger than life, arms spread to receive him.

"Over, over!"

A bird folded its wings and dove. Another, another, another—

Follow the guides, the Polyp said. *I won't fail you.*

Lyle aimed his crown and leaped, plunging headfirst, birds on either side.

8   *Child of Mine*

*Y*ou're safe. You're safe. I'm here, inside your head, Lyle, restoring the flow. Massaging your mind, removing blockages, opening the circuits."

The god's voice seemed low and elastic.

"I sound distorted because of the jolts you've taken," the Polyp explained. "Your memory, your grasp— Your vision clears quickly: your body, my blue arms emerging— All as clear as the sea."

"No. The danger is gone, for now."

Lyle turned, scanning the currents.

"And the Shark Saw too," the Polyp assured him.

"Can't you stop them?"

"I feel your distress," the Polyp said gently. "A god has his ways. The course is charted and my plan is in motion. You know Nawkoo's story, and you've seen his remains."

"Blednishev's hurt, the crew is desperate," Lyle protested. "These enemies—"

"Listen, please. We can put an end to them. I'm going to show you how."

All the Polyp's arms coiled at once.

"Relax," he said. "I'll guide your movements. Turn away from the surf and point your head down."

Lyle did as the Polyp asked, and they descended quickly, arrowing into the deep.

Across a broad canyon. Free, flying—

"Let the spirit of heaven fill you, Lyle. We'll trail our blue snakes behind and sample the current."

The far side came into view—a vertical wall. Lyle's heart was still hammering. The jolts were still ringing in his ears and his bones.

"Touch down and we'll wander along it. Feather fans wave from every shelf. Let them divert you."

Lyle lowered his lids momentarily, sending his mind into the tangle of arms, feeling their thickness, their movement, their tapered extremities. And when he opened his eyes, the arms were all his, reaching from his head like the spokes of a wheel, sweeping the rock, feeling the flow.

"A swarm of see-through baubles, glowing opals—globe-shaped creatures that clench as they drift. Ripple your snakes among them, enter their state. Time banished, and place. No up or down, no directional sense. Only detachment, abstraction. The end of gravity, the magic of floating in space.

"I remember them, Lyle. The day they emerged from these arms. Tentative they were—and still are—with an instinct for anonymity and a yearning for distance.

"Calmer?"

Calmer, Lyle thought. His fears were fading.

"A silver stream glitters ahead, winding toward us through curtains of pastel motes. Ray our arms into the school as it passes. Cometoids. Feel their natures—"

Tingles traveled the snakes. *Their natures*, Lyle thought. Speed, thrills, a focus that was constantly shifting.

"Like everything here," the Polyp said. "Emotion cast into flesh.

"Beneath our forearms—thimbles. They give me joy whenever I pass."

Twitching and attentive, rooted and accepting.

"Stroke their stipples, sniff their sweet dispositions. Stable, unchanged. But under that ledge, a rebel swarm brews. Taste the rancor?"

Lyle could taste it.

"A different breed. They're mobile, in a pique to be free. They've left the village, but they threaten no one. Hail them as we pass, and hope for the best."

Lyle sent his well wishes to the invisible creatures.

"Alright," the Polyp said. "Are you ready?"

"For what?"

"Evils, invaders— Moonholes and Saws, Spider Legs and the rest. We will treat them the same way I treat creatures gone wrong. That's what I'm going to show you— How I tend my gardens. How I judge, when I graft, what I prune and weed."

"Yes, I'm ready."

"Down," the Polyp directed him, "down the wall—

"Eye jellies pouched in the rock— Searching, rolling, peering through feather fans, forever curious— You can see why I treasure them.

"Spinner worms with fiery heads— Gray and vain, each spiked with a charge, buzzing their comrades, oppressing each other. The breadth of the sea is beyond their scope. They snap and spin without virtue or vision. But the zaps are an eyeful and the creatures bring life to the shelf. Shall I root them out?"

"Why do that?"

"Exactly," the Polyp said. "Energy and spirit is more than enough.

"Star acanthoids in piles, probes interwoven. Harmonious, purposeful, absorbed in their intricate designs. Fine creatures— But these crustaceous variations are headed in the wrong direction."

Lyle focused on the animals the Polyp was watching. Their probes were edged. Some had turned into claws.

"Shall I change them?" the god mused. "No. No force, not yet. A god too free with his power turns heaven to hell.

"But here— See it? Where the rock is perforated— something I really don't like."

Lyle drew closer. Creatures poked from every hole— tendrils, siphons, antennae, bending and sensing. Among them was a jagged rod, hardened to cut. Stiff and motionless.

"A fringe worm gone bad," the Polyp said.

"It looks like a weapon."

"It's becoming one," the Polyp said. "Touch him, Lyle. He can't hurt us."

Lyle ran an arm tip along the edge of the rod.

"I don't make predators," the Polyp told him. "Or parasites. I don't want them here. But every creature has the freedom to become what it wishes."

"Can you read its history?"

"No," the Polyp replied, "we can only guess what led it from the supple path, how this ugly calculus invaded its fabric."

"You can correct it?"

"We may not have to," the Polyp replied. "Use this arm, Lyle. Bind the worm. Uproot it, draw it out of the rock. Now—touch its soft parts. Send your mind into the struggling body and find its sick branches."

Lyle did as the Polyp asked. "I feel a numbness."

"And?"

"An itch, above his foot."

"Tension," Lyle read the sensations traveling his arm. "Impatience, scorn."

"The will to destroy," the Polyp divined. "He must be changed."

"He won't like that."

"No," the god agreed. "But if we don't make a change, he'll cause injury and death. And sicken the spirit of heaven."

"That would take a lot of bad worms."

"Not as many as you think," the Polyp said. "Carving salt requires patience and caution, doesn't it."

"What the tool cuts away," Lyle replied, "you can't put back. You learn to be careful."

"You must think before you act. Use your imagination to envision the outcome. And once the tool is in motion, you must be alert. Adapt to what you find, respond to surprises. You've made mistakes as a carver?"

"Of course."

"Such as—"

"I've overcarved pieces. Broken them. Ruined them by hurrying or poor concentration. Choosing the wrong thing to do with a tool, or failing to see what the tool would do."

"A god makes the same mistakes."

A frightening thought. "With lives," Lyle said.

"With lives."

The Polyp raised the fringe worm before them. "This isn't a piece of salt you can return to the rock pile. The procedure in this case is simple. My glands secrete a drop of sapphire fluid onto the back of your tongue."

Lyle watched an arm tip slide between his lips, felt it dip in the substance and return like a wetted brush.

"We will enter the creature here," the god said. "Right here. Be bold—pierce its flesh."

The worm stiffened. Lyle watched the arm sink into its foot, cutting and burning, moving with care and precision while it trembled and twitched.

"Excise the evil," the Polyp said, "and recircuit these nerves. Speak to it, Lyle: I'm making a change."

"I'm making a change," Lyle told the fringe worm.

"It hears you," the Polyp said, removing his arm. "We're finished. Set him down."

"This is how you change them? One at a time?"

"One at a time. It's the only way."

"And the change is permanent?"

"Not always," the Polyp answered. "Linkages grow back, foulness returns. Recircuiting may not be enough. That's next."

"Next?"

"At the rear of the shelf, the remnants of feather fans, bottle green and cream, protruding from chinks."

Lyle saw them. The fans looked like they'd been chewed to pieces.

"Listen."

Lyle heard a rasping sound.

"Look there—do you see?"

A bump of a creature was moving slowly along.

"Dragging his tongue beneath him," the Polyp said. "That's not how I designed him. He was built to strain his meals from the soup, like everyone else."

Lyle heard whimpers. A dying fan lay on the sand, clenching like a cat's paw. When Lyle touched it with an arm tip, its agony tore through him.

"A terrible thing," the Polyp said. "These beautiful creatures are being destroyed."

Lyle fixed on the rasper. "A predator."

"A fallen creature," the Polyp lamented.

"These are crimes," Lyle said.

"There are no crimes in heaven."

"You will punish the rasper."

"We deal out no punishments," the Polyp said, "and no rewards. We are here to create, to husband our creation, to protect our creatures from those who would threaten them.

"Shine the light of wisdom into the rasper, as you would a block of salt. See its weakness and strength, its flaws and its planes. The direction of its grain, where it drinks darkness and where the light passes through.

"Can you feel its nature, where preying has taken it?"

Lyle settled an arm on the rasper's back. The creature froze.

"Sloth," Lyle said, feeling its stupor. "Arrogance. And it's lost its sight."

"How might you change that?"

"Movement," Lyle answered. "Lift it from the floor, put it in flight."

"Those juvenile ruffle frills," the Polyp directed Lyle's gaze, "quivering like wings. Well, wings they can be. This one here would welcome the chance to see the world. But it will take some grafting."

One arm plucked the ruffle frills from the shelf. Another reached into Lyle's mouth and wet itself with fluid, while a third curled around the rasper.

The Polyp softened a spot on the rasper's back. "Go ahead, Lyle. Plant the roots of the ruffle frills here."

Lyle took control and put the frills in place, using the blue arms like sculpting tools.

"See there," the Polyp exclaimed. "Torpid, meet hyper. Senseless, meet acute."

The rasper's tongue shrank. Its body swelled as if it would burst. Then the clashing natures fused, and the hybrid launched into the current.

"Will the graft take?" Lyle wondered, watching it wing away.

"Will the discordant match be a withering branch?" the Polyp echoed his question. "Or a great tree of its own?

"Paradox, paradox— Song from sorrow, laughter from envy— If every creature knew the tale of its origin— Well then, none would see anything peculiar in me. But enough of salvation, enough remediation— If only our job was as simple as that. Down, farther down—"

Lyle dove and a plunging current caught them, arms snaking back like a flowing cape. The water's green grew deeper, murky and dark.

"Cressets," the Polyp directed Lyle's gaze.

bottom rose beneath them—low ridges divided by rivers of sand.

"Skim the bottom," the Polyp said, "sending our snakes to either side."

The sea life seemed sparse here, the water thick with silt.

"Death—can you taste it? Acrid—"

"Bitter," Lyle said. The surface before him was littered with curled bodies.

"Follow the trail," the Polyp directed.

"There—" A ghostly creature appeared through the haze, bearing a spiral shell on its back.

"A whorlitrap, Lyle. Insulated and aimless, sleepwalking, sunk in an anesthetic trance, like a Citizen lost in his tuner."

The creature's snout was crusted. Its shell was like armor, colorless and chalky.

"It spreads a fatal disease," the Polyp said. "Without knowing, it infects everything it touches. Our arms aren't immune, but they're numberless. Take hold of it."

Lyle circled the whorlitrap and lifted it up. "He's retreating, backing into his cell."

With a second arm, Lyle probed the opening, following the twisted corridor to a battered door. He could hear the animal wheezing behind it.

"Of the things that trouble me," the Polyp said, "this troubles me most. You see these poor innocents. Spinners, cometoids. Singing cats, choked and expiring. Cloisonias, hoods convulsed. All of them, the whorlitrap's victims."

"Shall I break into his home and pull him out?"

The Polyp was silent. And then, "There would be no point in that."

"Can't he be changed, like the predators?"

"Predators have a purpose to tinker with," the Polyp said. "The whorlitraps have none. The disease is woven into their nature."

"Can you confine him?"

"That's what I've done," the Polyp explained. "This is their infirmary, a corner of hell marked off in heaven."

"Do they know you?" Lyle asked.

"No," the god said. "And I don't know them. They're nothing at all like the creature I fashioned. They don't yearn for expression. They have nothing to express. The only desire they wish to fulfill is the one you see now. To return to their oblivion." The Polyp paused. "I'm being harsh."

"You're being foolish," Lyle said.

The Polyp was silent.

I've overstepped my bounds, Lyle thought.

"What would you do?" the Polyp asked.

"Pull him apart."

"He is ignorant of the death and contagion," the Polyp objected.

"And what of your children?" Lyle said. "Will you let the whorlitrap turn this sea into a grave for them? Will the Polyp's heaven become a desert, for the sake of creatures like this?" He pried at the whorlitrap's door, half-expecting the Polyp to stop him. He bound the cowering whorlitrap and yanked him out. The Polyp said nothing.

With a pair of arms, Lyle clasped the animal broadside and ripped him down the middle. Again he divided him, and again, until the creature was nothing but twitching pieces.

Lyle felt the Polyp's reaction, his shock and wonder. Then he heard his voice, distant and strangely wistful.

145

"Nawkoo, through and through," the god said.

The arms that held the whorlitrap's remains were splotched and pale. Lyle stared at them, loosing his grip. The pieces fell to the sand.

"Leave them here," the Polyp said. "Hurry—"

The god took command of Lyle's body, grappling the sea floor and pulling with his arms, swinging behind the lee of a reef. Then he drew the snakes back, out of sight.

"Evil breeds evil," the Polyp said. "I taste another flesh-eater nearby—one that preys on both living and dead."

Lyle peered through the veils of drifting silt.

"The struggle and the scent of blood lures him out," the Polyp said.

From a ragged hole, a pair of giant claws rose. The light of the cressets glinted on their razor edges.

"A scourge-of-claws," the Polyp said.

"Your creation?" Lyle asked with amazement.

"Gone very wrong," the god affirmed. "I've destroyed most of them. There aren't many left."

"It's holding on to—"

"An agonized finscribe and struggling antennil," the Polyp said.

As they watched, the claws tightened, crushing the fin-scribe, cutting the antennil in two. The jointed arms delivered their prey to the mechanical jaws.

"No bond, no connection," the Polyp lamented. "No sympathy for the lives it takes. The scourge feels nothing."

Its eyes were glassy and faceted. Its rigid legs clacked as it

sidled toward them. Big as a man, it squatted over the whorlitrap pieces and began to feed.

"Prepare yourself," the Polyp said.

The blue arms whipped, and Lyle was whirled from the
lee, approaching the scourge from behind, snakes extended.

"I'm growing, Lyle, and you're growing with me."

In a heartbeat, Lyle was two, three, four times larger. His
arms lashed the scourge, startling it, circling its carapace,
lifting it easily. There were knobs on the creature's back. It
erected them, driving them into his middle. Claws grappled
his sides—

"Don't let go," the Polyp said.

The scourge twisted to free itself, frenzied, scrabbling,
lime joints crackling, whorlitrap gurry dribbling from its jaws.
A claw scissored at Lyle's head. Another snapped at his snakes,
razoring through one.

"Don't let go, don't—"

They tumbled over the furrowed sea floor, raising clouds.
The scourge caught another arm, slicing through it. It was
face-on now, stabbing Lyle's trunk, stalked eyes glaring,

"Upend it, raise it—"

Lyle gripped the scourge in a dozen places and lifted. It
rose from the sand.

"Higher, higher! Now bring it down—"

Lyle bashed the scourge's chassis against the floor. A spiracle in its brow dilated and a pulse of venom stung his face.
Lyle's legs wobbled.

"Poison can't stop the blue snakes. Circle your arms—all of them, all of them! Squeeze, Lyle, squeeze—"

With the scourge in his arms, Lyle squeezed. He heard the case crack. The jointed legs thrashed. Squeezing, cracking— More venom, a claw at Lyle's neck—

"Squeeze!"

Lyle used all his strength, and the rigid body collapsed like a broken egg.

The claws relaxed.

Lyle released his holds, and the creature rolled onto its entrails, a heap of curdled slime. The hiss of the spiracle died, and the light in its eyes sputtered out.

"Our birds," the god alerted him.

A gang of torpedoes were weaving around them.

"Summoned to a meal," the Polyp said.

Darting and stretching their snake-like necks, the picket birds dismembered the scourge and consumed it.

"We have wounds," the Polyp said.

Lyle gazed at the severed arms. Blood flowed from them, midnight blue. The three the whorlitrap infected were white, withered and limp.

"We sluff them," the Polyp told him.

As Lyle watched, they detached at their bases, dissolving as the current bore them away.

"And from the roots—"

Five new arms congealed.

"Predators, parasites, the debased and debauched, psychos and sloths— The miscreants in heaven are few. But among

148

the fallen worlds, there are gardens of evil so choked by weeds that no tending is possible. Life must be destroyed and started anew."

"The people of Salt," Lyle said. "You killed them all."

"I won't speak of that now," the Polyp replied. "But you will have an answer. Very soon. Point your head toward the canyon wall. Up, Lyle. To brighter climes. We're giant now, we rise quickly.

"It's time to show you the purest act."

Creation, Lyle thought.

"Creation," the god echoed, "from scratch. A vacant place—that's all we need. And plenty of room. There—"

They were gliding toward a naked cove lit by cressets. As they approached, the Polyp's blue arms turned spongy. Pinholes, tackholes and pits appeared. The skin began to bubble, and as Lyle watched, the bubbles burst, leaving large pores. From the pores, strange parts emerged—muscle knots, cysts and burls.

"For the cove, the cove—"

The blue arms were swelling like bellies packed with born, wriggling and alive.

"Spin, Lyle, spin!

"Swell and release, swell and release— Each pore a horn of plenty—"

They were whirling, arms wide, painting the walls with a bedlam of life.

"Creatures that roll and crawl and are planted and fly.

Head-feathered, frog-lipped, sleek and sectioned; nacreous, neon, figured and striped; hanging, jiggling, clinging with glowing villi; tossed, clapping, stroking and finning in every direction.

"A myriad tempers, each with a future coiled within."

Lyle was shaking from head to foot, heart in his throat. *The flow, the flow*— The divine release, spawn of spirit and mind—his deepest desire, his dream come to life.

Inside you, he thought. The god was a churning womb. *They were all inside you.*

"Inside *us*," the Polyp said.

The blue arms hung limp, pores closing, skin sealing over.

"To each of our offspring we've given our body, our thoughts, our blood. But even as we watch, the infants claim their independence. Lids crack, frosted eyes turn. Knots unknot, stalks unfurl, antennae quiver and turn. The coruscations subside, colors lodging in the submarine light, patterns decided."

Lyle watched the creatures disperse. Some sought a place on the wall, some fell to the sand and burrowed in, some had already vanished in the turbulent sea.

"I never imagined—"

"Rise," the Polyp said. "Make for the surface."

Lyle aimed his crown and eeled the blue arms.

"As we ascend, you return to man-size. Our people—see them?"

The wall was thronged.

"They're waving from pockets, emerging from crannies,

leaning from ledges to cheer what we've done. On the ramparts, a hundred feather fans waving. Cloisonias flashing on shelves, their vibrating hoods bathing us in elysian scents. Klensiars mouthing, anemones and velvet rings swelling as we pass— Glorying in the life their god's given them, and the portion they shaped for themselves."

A wealth of scents and sounds, sights and sensations reached Lyle through the snaking arms.

"You're responding to my jewels."

"And the artistry of their author," Lyle said.

"Heaven is a wonderful place." The Polyp spoke with a note of sadness.

"Your children are grateful, and so is your student."

"You are far more than that."

"A god can make whatever companion he likes."

"An enigma, I know," the Polyp replied. "What draws the father of heaven to an apostate of hell?"

Above, submarine arches appeared. They were smooth and blue, a sculpture of snakes carved out of rock. And the red profusions gushing from the spans, sprouting from their shoulders.

"Plume irises," the Polyp said.

The arches were ablaze with them, turning in the currents on quaking stalks, horns stretching and flaming scarlet to gold.

"Stream your arms through them, Lyle. Feel them quicken, remembering. Life for them started with you. They're opening, showing their tubes."

Lyle circled the stalks with a dozen arms. "Soft."

"So soft," the Polyp echoed. "Squeeze and shake them while your body twists free in the flow. It's love, love they're expressing—"

The horn before Lyle's face flared, its insides rayed with golden striations. Then it sucked its tube back and eviscerated in a miracle of sound and color.

The bloom drowned his senses. "Are you with me?"

"I'm right here," the Polyp said. "Release your hold and let the current carry us."

They passed through a spray of strikers that glittered like silver pins.

"If anything—" The Polyp swallowed his words.

An atomic shower, a whispering mist. Nests of flossworms, glassy, wriggling—

"If anything should happen to you—"

"You're thinking of him," Lyle said.

The Polyp was quiet. Then he murmured, "Can you feel the chill in this forlorn current?"

"It was hard, when he died."

"I died with him," the god said. "I felt his death in all my parts."

"And after he was gone?"

"When there was no spark left, when I had no choice but to leave, I bore my immortality like a curse."

"He was a fighter," Lyle said.

"Because he came from a world like Salt, and because he was a man—a predator, a fallen creature—I tasted life's tragedy through him. How fear destroys wonder, beauty becomes camouflage, and the child is forced into hiding. I learned what rage is. And how a man uses a god's power."

A triggerbill threesome passed. Then a galaxy wheeling with tiny striped cups and translucent balloons.

"He changed you," Lyle said.

"Yes, he did."

The current grew stronger. On the wall, rip whisks thrashed, the rooted sea trees waving like palms in a monsoon.

"I'm not Nawkoo," Lyle said.

"My mourning is over."

"But something darkens your thoughts. The Shark Saw, Spider Legs— You're afraid they'll destroy me."

"No. We'll prevail."

"What then?" Lyle asked.

"You're mortal. I would lose you, as I lost him."

The canyon ended. They were swept around a buttress. The Polyp spread his blue arms and they coiled around Lyle like pinwheel tracers. Then an upwelling caught them, and they were shooting skyward. Lyle could see a blurred sun through the liquid ceiling. They passed a shallow shelf packed with life. Nested ruffle fans. Jellies violet and rose. Finscribes etched with a master's tool, scarlet, emerald, opalescent blue, with enamalids curled between them. The Polyp was retracting his snakes.

"Don't."

"What does that mean?" the Polyp asked.

The picket birds appeared around them. Above, the disk of the sun was bending and stretching on the water's surface.

"I don't want to go back."

"You must go back," the Polyp said.

"Stay with me."

"Stay? For a minute, an hour?"

"Don't ever leave," Lyle replied.

"The blue snakes fan," the Polyp said gently, "raying from your head like an alien sun. The shadow of the *Mithostra* approaches. I'm calling it to us.

"You know why you were taken to the gravehouse. You learned about the life Nawkoo led, and you saw how it ended."

The prow of the *Mithostra* divided the currents, nosing down. Its hull was combed by worms and lined with thimbles. Its hawsehole shifted like a giant eye. The ship seemed to yawn, moaning, sucking water into its jaws.

Lyle felt the pull. It was suddenly fierce.

He was sliding through the ship's echoing gullet, into her cavernous hold.

9 Something Greater

The Custodial Center to which Lyle was taken was in a manufacturing district at the south end of the city. It was surrounded by high block walls and patrolled round-the-clock by Security soldiers. In the mid afternoon of his second day of confinement, Lyle was escorted by an armed guard down a well-lit corridor. The walls were white and the chlorite tiles were wafered like the scales of a quarry lizard. Lyle wore white penal overalls and manacles. The guard directed him into a small holding pen.

Inside the pen, Minister Audrie stood by an interrogation table with a Custody warden. Jordan was at attention by the door. Lyle fixed on the Minister. Audrie looked at his folded hands while the warden spoke.

To Lyle's surprise, the warden explained that he was being released "on the Minister's recognizance." The guard removed

Lyle's manacles, and when the warden left the pen, the guard followed.

"They're allowing me to remove you," the Minister said, looking up. "I had to post my children as bond," he said wryly.

Lyle was silent and sullen, but amazed nonetheless. They were freeing him?

"I pled your case at a high level," the Minister told him. "The highest." He shook his head as if he questioned the wisdom of what he'd done.

"I understand," Audrie said. "You felt betrayed. But what happened was beyond my control. The Preserve was scrapped, the entire gorge was condemned, and I was the last to know. We weren't going to change the fate of that place. I'm sorry. I tried."

Lyle looked the Minister over. His hair was carefully combed. He was wearing the white suit with a white flower on the pocket. "You don't care about the Wells. You were lying to me then, and you're lying to me now. Your people were setting up a live broadcast. It was probably your idea."

"What do you know?" Audrie burst out, face flushing with anger. "The show was the Chief's idea. If I'm so mean-spirited, why am I here? Why am I gambling my future to free you?"

He raised his hands as if calling a truce, then he circled the table.

"Lyle," Audrie said gently. "I wish I didn't have to tell you this. Your mother's not well." He put his hand on Lyle's shoulder.

Lyle felt weak. He saw the compassion in the Minister's eyes.

"The shock of your arrest," Audrie told him.

"Where is she?"

"At home."

"Can I see her?" Lyle asked.

"Of course."

The door of the pen squealed open. Lyle turned to see a tall middle-aged woman in a white coat step toward him. He'd never seen her in the flesh, but like everyone in the land of Salt, he knew the Doctor from her broadcasts. Her blond hair was swept back from her brow, braided at the rear in a rope that hung over one shoulder. Her nose was bold, with snagged nostrils.

The Minister smiled, as if he was greatly pleased by her arrival.

"This is—"

"Doctor Wentt," the woman introduced herself. She offered her hand.

Lyle shook it.

She wore her coat open, and the neckline of her dress was low, revealing a chest without breasts. Her eyes had an affable glow.

"The destruction of State property is a Grade Four offense," Wentt said, "and the demonstration of malice prohibits a pardon." She put a hand on her hip. "There can be no sentence indulgence, no merit reductions, no amnesty. An officer of the

State," she nodded at Audrie, "has requested a temporary suspension of the proceedings against you, and the request has been granted. Therefore—" She cocked her head. "Your future is in his hands."

She smiled. "He's asked me to play a role." Her ring finger crookt. "Your case has garnered a lot of air time. I missed the blasting show, but I hear it may top the ratings this year." The thumb quivered and the forefinger lifted. Her digits seemed to operate independently of each other. "They enjoy a spectacle, don't they."

"Nothing was done to glorify the crime," the Minister pointed out.

"Of course not," Wentt smiled. Without warning, her cordiality dissolved. "Something has come up," she told Audrie. "Can we get this over now?"

"Please—" The Minister was flustered. "Let's proceed as we—"

"Get what over?" Lyle asked.

"Alright." Wentt gave the Minister a nod of assent.

Then she turned and exited the pen.

It was the middle of his working day, but the Minister had Jordan drive them to the villa. When they arrived, he excused his attaché and asked the kitchen staff to retire. He seated Lyle at the counter and prepared a small meal for the two of them, speaking all the while. This was their business, their challenge, he said. They needed to do whatever had to be done to put the Wells behind them.

Afterward, Audrie led him to the workroom. The sight of the space, and the sculptures awaiting his return, had an impact on Lyle. And on the Minister as well. He said little, seemed content to breathe the odors and touch the tools. But as they were leaving, he grasped Lyle's arm. "We were happy here," he said.

From there, they followed the paths around the villa grounds. The Minister talked at length about a return to the way things had been. Lyle sensed a hidden motive, but when he pressed him, Audrie went quiet. The sun was low on the horizon when he led Lyle onto the spacious veranda overlooking the city.

As they scanned the metropolis, the foothills and the white ridges in the distance, Audrie chose that moment to strike a deeper chord.

"I loved your work from the first moment I saw it," he said. "That first day we met— I loved your spirit. You're the son I never had."

He took a breath. "I've done everything I can to help you. You don't have any way of knowing the kind of pressure I'm under. But I've risked my future, and my family's future— for you.

"With some State matters, my voice isn't heard. You have the evidence of that. But I wield a lot of power. And I'm not afraid to use it."

He faced Lyle with an expression that was part optimism,

part resignation. "There are great things we can do together. A sequence of moves, carefully planned— We can remake this world. But it can't be entirely on our terms. We have to meet it halfway."

He sighed, and then laughed at his gravity. "Look, can you see it? It's always like that at this time of day."

Lyle scanned the city, uncertain what he meant.

"The sun strikes his front," the Minister pointed. "It's full in his face."

He was gazing at the statue of the patriarch in Memorial Park.

"How many eyes are on him right now?" Audrie wondered. "How many will watch the sun rise and set, and the seasons change around him, this month and this year?" He regarded Lyle and nodded. "It's a powerful thing—that statue."

A feared future opened to Lyle.

"You dream of the sea," the Minister said. "I too have a dream—a worldly one. I dream of being the Chief, and giving Salt a new soul. These dreams, and our fates, can be joined. The future can be ours. Together. That's what I want."

Audrie turned back to the statue. Lyle was silent.

"A sequence of moves," the Minister said. "I'm the Chief's darling right now. In time, he's going to choose me as his successor. Imagine: Memorial Park with a statue at either end. The leader from the past, our patriarch; and the Chief, a leader whose achievements cry out to be honored—facing each other. Both with an arm extended. A compact, a handshake across the years."

There was a hint of irony in the Minister's voice.

"You've shared this with him?"

Audrie turned, eyeing him darkly. "It's all a fantasy, without you."

"It would keep me out of prison," Lyle guessed.

Audrie nodded. "You'd become one of us. A Helper. We'd work on the details together—you and I."

"The Chief likes the idea?"

"Loves it," Audrie murmured. "A vain dog he is. He'll be posing for you—you'll see."

"And my crime?"

"Gone," Audrie waved his hand. "I had hoped to spring the statue on him after you and I fleshed it out. But with you in custody, I had to spoil the surprise."

Lyle heard voices. Jordan was leading a woman out from the shade of the veranda. It was Doctor Wentt. She was in clinical attire, and the white lab coat billowed behind her. She spotted Lyle and then looked away.

"Don't let her intimidate you," Audrie said. "The arrangement's done."

Wentt threw up before the Minister had a chance. "It's dramatic," she smiled, taking in the view. "'He has taste.' That's what he says about you."

Audrie waved the compliment aside. "You do the hard work. Someone has to keep us in line. Thanks for taking the time—"

"Not at all. I want to be closer to Culture."

"Well," Audrie glanced at Lyle, "shall we?"

Wentt faced the young sculptor, but her eyes took a while to find him. "I wish we'd spoken beforehand," she said to the Minister.

"Corinne—"

"The special treatment troubles me," Wentt said. "I'm trying to make crime unfashionable."

North of the villa, the salt hills rose one behind the other. In the oblique light, Lyle could see wave and ripple patterns. It was as if the dead hills were dreaming of life.

"We have the same goal," Audrie assured the Doctor.

"That's important," Wentt said, settling on Lyle.

"The Chief's tribunal has approved a Forbearance decree," she explained in a more formal voice. "It's conditional. If you accept Minister Audrie's offer and become a Helper, if you perform the tasks he defines and you commit no further crimes, you will become an employee of Culture. If you fail to meet any of these conditions, you will become a prisoner of the State." She switched her head to point her words. "Your sentence is thirty years. If you decide to serve it, you will return to Custody, and will remain there until your term is complete.

"Do you understand the choice you're being given?"

Lyle nodded.

"Good," the Minister smiled. "I think that covers it."

"Have you discussed my suggestion with him?" the Doctor asked.

"The public apology? Not yet," Audrie replied. "You must join us for dinner some evening."

"I would enjoy that," Wentt said, turning to face the villa.

"Jordan?" the Minister spoke to his tuner. "Would you show Doctor Wentt to the door."

Jordan appeared and escorted her away.

Audrie exhaled with a taxed expression. "Could you smell it?" he fanned the air by his nose. "She must have come directly from some butchery."

"A cold woman," Lyle said.

"In her book, every lawbreaker is a dissident. A threat to the State. She views Culture as an appeasement. A concession to—"

Just then the Minister was interrupted by a call on his tuner. He turned his shoulder to Lyle, and when he turned back, his features were grave.

"Your mother," he said. "She's had a stroke. You'd better go." And then, "I'm trusting you, Lyle."

He had passed the new high-rise zone and was descending into the clutter of shacks and shanties he'd called home for so many years. A half-dozen children were playing in the road, and as Lyle approached, one remembered him. "The man who carved animals at the Museum." Lyle stopped to catch his breath.

"Make us one," a boy said. He picked up a hunk of rock salt from beside the road and handed it to him.

"Not right now. Later—I promise."

163

"They used to live in Fossil Wells," a little girl said.

"Yes, they did." Lyle touched her cheek. He knelt and scanned the powdered faces. "Animals love water," he said, "because it never stops moving. It's free and it flows," he fished his hand past their eyes, "and it just keeps flowing. Movement makes water happy, and it makes us happy too."

The little girl nodded.

"I promise," Lyle repeated. Then he rose and hurried toward home.

A minute later the shack appeared through the shadows. Perhaps it was the dusk or the diminished importance of his parents in his life, but the dwelling looked smaller than it ever had before. Lyle knocked on the door and entered.

His father was seated in the front room, ten feet away. He rose slowly and they embraced.

"How is she?" Lyle asked.

His father pursed his lips. "See for yourself." He gestured toward the bedroom.

The sagging mattress and his mother asleep—a familiar sight. But what Lyle saw as he approached the bed wasn't familiar at all. Was she awake or asleep? It was hard to tell. Her eyes were open, her lips were parted as if she was about to speak. But her face was frozen, runneled and creased like the dead sea's floor. He reached for her hand and then stopped himself. It lay beside her like a foreign object, crooked and white.

He grabbed hold of it, tears wetting his cheeks.

Who was he crying for? Did she know he was there? It was then, with the prospect of losing her clearly before him, that Lyle realized how much he had counted on her strength and support. Despite his fears for her health and her life, he had hoped she could still give him that.

"How long has she been like this?"

"A couple of hours," his father replied. "The medics just left."

"What did they do?"

"She couldn't breathe. I called the Minister. He had them dispatched."

"He's no friend of ours," Lyle said.

"I'm thankful for his help," his father bristled. "They saved her life."

Lyle turned, surprised by the anger.

"It was the news about you that did this," the aging man said.

Lyle shook his head, unable to speak.

"Why, Lyle? Do you have to set yourself against everyone?"

He faced his father's grief, feeling how far he'd traveled from home. He was dangerous now, not just to himself. The Minister had a part in all of this. Audrie had been talking to his father with the statue in mind.

"He's arranged things for all of us," Lyle muttered.

"He's trying to help you," his father said, sorely vexed. "Why can't you take his guidance? He has a good name and many successes. What more do you want?"

Lyle stood facing him, the words echoing in his head. Then he bent over the bed, kissed his mother's brow and whispered goodbye.

His father followed him out of the bedroom.

"You can stay here if you like," his father said.

Lyle paused before the alcove where he'd slept, seeing his old pack beside the bed. The one he'd first taken into Fossil Wells. He knelt and opened it. The hardware was there, ropes and hammer, as if he'd set it down the day before.

"I can use this," he said, slinging it on his back.

He glanced at his cot and shook his head at his father.

When they reached the front door, the aging man grasped his arm. "Erla always saw your side," he said despondently. "Forgive me, son."

"I understand," Lyle replied.

Above him, clouds were tumbling like surf, the curls gilded. When Lyle lifted his head, water dripped from his chin. He touched his neck.

The blue arms had vanished.

He was in the ship's stern, wrapped in his blanket. Blednishev was seated beside him. The magic and turmoil of the submarine realm, the power he'd known when the Polyp was close— Lyle felt like an animal that had been given his freedom and then forced back into his cage.

In the west, the swamped sun was torching the sea. The

deck of the *Mithostra* gleamed. Water was pooled by the companionway, and the foot of the wheelhouse was soaked. The outlines of his salt figurines had melted and real creatures lay scattered among them. Sand lollies were tangled in the guys, bottom buttons clung to the bulwarks, anemones dotted the planks.

"The cabin and hold are flooded," Blednishev said. He sounded tentative, wary. His coat was fastened over his wound.

Lyle peered into the seaman's eyes. The wind knocked the knotted end of a rope against a scupper, marking off time.

"You've arrived," Blednishev said.

The urgent journey, their mission, their goal— Where was the Polyp?

Lyle got his feet beneath him and stood.

The ship was at anchor, riding the swells, playing out chain and pulling it taut. Picket birds lined the rails. A blue cliff rose sheer to starboard, and the sea crashed against it.

Blednishev was up now, standing beside him. Alfred approached, stripped to the waist. "We're ready," he said.

Lyle looked at the native and then at Blednishev. Ready

Alfred on his right. The two circled his back with their arms and urged him forward. He moved with them, past the cabin, along the gunnel.

As they approached the bow, Lyle saw smoke and flames.

Gobo was kneeling on the foredeck, bare-chested. Keetch, wearing only boots and cape, fed the wood he'd chopped to a mounting fire. Lantern candles were piled beside him, along with bowls and pans. A pot with something bubbling in it rested on the coals.

"There," Keetch pointed at a spot.

Blednishev and Alfred led Lyle to it.

"Toward the fire, with your back to the cabin."

Lyle turned, feeling the heat on his face.

"Sit," Keetch said.

Lyle lowered himself, and Alfred sank beside him. Blednishev sat in the space between Gobo and Keetch. The horizon was red now, the sky darkening.

"Our wax of change," Keetch spoke to the fire.

Gobo and Alfred watched Lyle through narrowed lids, from a vanishing point. Blednishev stared at the flames.

Keetch placed the remaining candles in the bubbling pot. A burst of embers, and the blaze eddied up. He grunted and lifted his arms, and the other two natives did the same, hooking the air with their hands. The shadows on the planking opened and closed like curled claws.

Keetch dipped his fingers into the pot and lifted them to his face. Painting it with wax.

Now Alfred and Gobo. Smeared, sagging, shapeless masks—

"Soot," Keetch croaked.

The three bent forward, faces to the fire, and the wax turned black. Then they were pinching and trenching, shaping their features. Gobo's forehead turned ropy, brow jutting, eyes sunk in deep sockets. His lips were pushed out as from a wind blasting through them. Alfred's nostrils arched, cheeks

168

grooved, chin pointed. Keetch sealed over one of his eyes. The lumps on his brow were small heads emerging. He worked with only his left hand now. The right arm shook, rattling the bracelet.

From Gobo's bugled lips, whistles and whines. From Alfred's, gasps and glubs, like a man underwater. Lyle watched, filled with foreboding. *Change*— Some new state of flesh or mind. A new shock, about to be delivered.

All at once the three natives began to shake as if struck by some nervous disease. Alfred scissored his limbs. Gobo stooped, humpbacked. Keetch's head wagged to free itself from his neck. Lyle's heart was racing, he struggled for breath. The racket mounted, the three natives raving as one. And then—

The captain's bell rang.

Something was pulling on the rope in the flooded cabin.

Keetch stood.

Lyle watched him lurch toward the companionway, heard the slosh of his boots as he descended. The bell continued, a measured tolling. Gobo and Alfred were silent, frozen in the flickering light. Lyle imagined the Polyp hovering in the cabin below, his hair floating on the captain's pillow, blue arms snaking over the drowned bed.

The tolling stopped. Splashing—

Keetch was returning, climbing the ladder.

Gobo pulled a charred stake from the fire and drummed on the foredeck, goosenecking and gabbling like a picket bird. Alfred grabbed another, turned a pot over and raised a hollow *pang-pang*. Blednishev sat motionless, watching.

The fire crackled. Behind Lyle, boots jarred the planks.
He fought the temptation to turn.

Is it you? Lyle thought.

He heard the Polyp's answer in his ears and his mind.

"Close your eyes."

Lyle closed them.

"Human bonds," the Polyp said, "are tenuous, ephemeral—"

A god can secure them, Lyle thought.

"Can a god compel devotion? From a flossworm or a man? Are my creatures devoted to me? Am I devoted to them? Lyle, Lyle—

"We are devoted to our own aspirations—whoever has hold of them.

"Don't turn. My renegade. My renegade from the Land of Salt.

"I want you to stand.

"Pull the blanket from your shoulders.

"It's a victor I see, glittering with sweat, his stripes lit by the fire. The cold air touches you. And now Keetch bends at the waist. His hands reach out, and you feel a chill where he's touched you. A crawling sensation. Expanding, climbing your back. I'm working my arms around you. A shiver, and my hub moves onto your shoulder.

"You're afraid."

I am.

A rustle of wings.

"The picket birds rise from their perches, batting and gathering close, alighting on the deck around you, wings raised, tips touching."

The Polyp topped his shoulder. Lyle felt him slide onto his chest.

"Keetch falls to his knees," the god said. "Alfred and Gobo huddle on either side, pressing their waxed cheeks to the planks by your feet.

"Relax your jaw— It will be different this time."

Different—

"'Don't ever leave,' you said." The god spoke slowly. "Think what that means."

Lyle felt the roots of a great joy stirring inside him, emotions of a heart much larger than his own.

"Open your eyes," the Polyp said. "Look into mine."

Lyle parted his lids. The pinpricks pierced him. The silver gyres were turning.

"Will this be the last time?" the god asked.

The last time we are two, Lyle read his mind.

"A man's life is finite," the god said. "This will be all of it.

The ship and the natives were silent, and so was the sea. The picket birds were still as stone.

Lyle raised his hands, placed them on either side of the Polyp's bell.

He lifted the soft mass, gathering the tangled limbs, drawing the god closer.

Your pupil no more, he thought. *Tonight I lead.*

He parted his lips, guiding the Polyp toward them, feeling the blue mass shifting between his palms. The god touched his tongue, and then he was crawling over it, sliding through the portal at the back of his throat.

"I'm inside you now."

Forever? For good?

"For the rest of your life," the god assured him.

The welling in Lyle's center burst, and a fountain rose within him. A flood of gladness— His heart cried out.

"I'm mounting your brain, riding forward—"

"Arms," Lyle said, "your arms—"

"I've found the cleared passages. My arms eel through them, whispering, weaving—your knives and files, your numberless tools— Look around you, Lyle."

The snakes were emerging, coiling into the air on either side, winding down his chest and over his shoulders like living braids.

"I arch my middle," the Polyp said softly, "squeezing my menisci, bathing my underside in sapphire fluid. And now— I'm melting, nestling down, bonding my hub and the roots of my arms to this eager brain."

A spasm ran down Lyle's spine, into his depths.

"The fusing has taken," the Polyp told him.

Lyle felt the change in his body. And along with it, a calm that surrounded him and the tangle of arms like a glittering cloud. Home for a god's thoughts. Billows in which a dream of heaven might live—

The waters beneath the ship were paling. A glow from the deep was rising toward them.

"To fete our union," the Polyp said. "A swarm of antennils, clicking and luminescent, pulsing brighter as the moment approaches to affirm our purpose."

"Our purpose." Lyle felt the Polyp's thoughts mingling with his own as the frenzied swarm rose, blue arms rippling and flashing as the light grew brighter.

"Tonight, right now—"

"Tonight, right now," Lyle repeated.

"We make the solemn vow."

"The solemn vow."

"To give ourselves to something greater."

Heaven, Lyle thought. *Its teeming walls, lush gardens, the blood of free currents—* "To something greater."

"Your arms, my arms," the Polyp intoned.

"My mind and yours."

"Lord of the sea," the Polyp said softly.

"Lord of the sea," Lyle echoed with pride.

"Creator."

"Creator," Lyle said.

10 Give Me Strength

The swells rose suddenly. The ship bucked beneath Lyle. A wind aft, a fierce blast— The anchor chain snapped. Alfred and Gobo clung to the deck. Blednishev gripped the rail, watching with a knowing smile. The ship was careening, lines humming as the water spiked. Without a hand on the wheel, they were angling forward.

What's happening? Lyle thought.

Rain was falling in big, cold drops.

"Look around you," the Polyp said.

Peaks were jutting from the waves, their tops boiling white. Over the stern, Lyle could see them coming.

"This is your element," the god said. "Lift your blue arms and ride the tide."

At Lyle's beck, the arms rose. The blaze cast his shadow on the waters, his head a writhing medusa, snakes kinking and coiling in every direction.

175

"Your chest is heaving, your frame is shaking," the Polyp said. "And the ship shakes with you, coming alive."

The planks trembled, the hull groaned— The *Mithostra* lurched as if her side had been struck. The mainmast swayed through a curtain of spray, ropes jumping, spars creaking. The natives were prostrate. Blednishev moved grip by grip amidships.

"To the prow," the Polyp directed.

Lyle reached with his eels. They whipped around stanchions, scuppers, the hatch, getting hold of the windlass— The ship's hind sank as a wave crashed over it, and the stern dissolved, surge sweeping the deck. The picket birds rose en masse, thrashing their wings.

The *Mithostra* was headed up a steep slope. She shivered at the top and pierced a curl as it broke over her bow. Water charged down, dashing against Lyle's knees, jerking him around. It struck Alfred full force, lifting him, arms spread, neck twisted, legs clear of the deck. He blurted like a picket bird and turned into one, slicing the air, free of the ship, wings fanning to catch the wind.

The running flood swerved as the port side rolled, foaming toward Gobo and Keetch. The big man danced on the froth, arms sprouting feathers, while Keetch spread his cape and kicked off his boots, waxed face stretching—wide-eyed, hook-beaked. An urgent gabble and they took wing together, Gobo heading into the side of a wave and emerging behind it, Keetch climbing steeply to join the birds wheeling above.

A shriek, the mainmast tore free of its collar and crashed

over the cabin, smashing the roof, shattering windows and crushing the inflatable. Blednishev was huddled against a wrecked wall, and as the ship sluffed the ruins, he slid into the sea.

Lyle reached for him, blue arms eeling, searching the churn, coiling around him— But the seaman slid through. His gray oilskins had a sapphire gleam, lit from beneath by the antennil swarm. As Lyle watched, the gleaming legs dwindled, trunk rippling, neck stretching, Blednishev's head like a buoy on a line.

"Dissolving," the Polyp said.

Blednishev was a spill of the transforming fluid, oily and shimmering. Blobs and jots in a wandering slurry— Now only his head remained.

The thick lips twitched and smiled at Lyle. His eyes were pleased and his fondness shone through—a moment of sentiment, now that his duty was set aside.

The glistening guise stretched and joined the ship's wake.

"My solace, my refuge," the Polyp said.

Beneath Lyle's feet, the deck gave. It was rubbery skin, emerged from its silver-green side. The ship dipped into the surge, the last of its nautical dressings swept clear. As it surfaced, a notched tail lifted forty feet in the air.

"The mounting waves no longer pound us," the Polyp said. "Som Thoosy rides them with ease."

The head of the sea beast twisted. Lyle saw an eye rolling in a rubbery socket.

"Hang on."

Som's speckled jaws parted and a gray tongue emerged, quivering as a groan echoed deep in her gullet. She turned half around, heaving up— And the sea rose with her, a blue mountain erupting with a silver giant inside, headed for the stars.

Lyle was frozen in midair, sheets of water crashing down—

"Now let go," the Polyp said.

Lyle's arms went limp, and Som hurled him from her nose. Arcing through the darkness, he saw her spine curve as she dove back in and the waves washed over her. Then he plunged into the churn, and was caught in her suck and dragged down.

Tumbled and crunched, snagged and splayed. Down and down, the clicking antennils in a frenzy around him.

"The drag is releasing you," the Polyp said.

As the suck subsided and the light pulsed brighter, Lyle could see a submarine canyon with towering spires. Som passed between two pinnacles and disappeared.

"The currents are strong."

An upwelling rose beneath Lyle, and as rapidly as he'd plunged, he was borne back to the surface, furled and smothered with claps of foam. *Shark Saw*, Lyle thought. He was in open water.

The Polyp was silent.

The waves were enormous, crosscurrents colliding, piling into high walls. Lyle slid into a trough and there was no seeing out of it. He rode up its slope and whirled over its crest. Then the peak caught him and hurled him down.

Defenseless, lifted up, hurled down. Up and down again, body battered and wrenched, tugged and stretched—

"Strength," the Polyp whispered.

Something was pounding inside him, battering to make room.

"Find it, Lyle."

He struggled to regain the surface as the hammering mounted, shaking his core, stretching his ribcage till he thought it would burst.

"Fight, fight—"

Lyle fought with his limbs—all of them, blue and human—warding off panic while the god hissed in his ear.

"Find your strength—"

Were the waves laying back? The surge seemed weaker, but still fierce enough to force him down. Again the water sealed over him, he was doubled, rolling— But slowly, more slowly. Was the sea settling?

"You are growing," the Polyp said.

Lyle's trunk was thicker, his head weighty. His blue arms were tangled, cumbrous, inflating—

"Stand, Lyle. Stand—"

His feet touched the bottom. He lifted his shoulders, and the combing currents slid over them.

Air met his lips as his head cleared the surface—chest quaking, still growing—glimpsing from a new elevation the cliffs of heaven and the luminescent sea. The pelting rain was a veil of gauze, the tossing waves a delicate stippling.

"Your shoulders soar, a ridgeline of their own."

He was growing, growing, head towering above the peaks. Enormous blue serpents twisted over his shoulders, down his chest and belly, while threads of picket birds circled his cheeks. He stood on the sea floor, thigh-deep in a lake of light—a naked giant, painted with red rivers. And inside his head, gyri and fissures the size of mountains and inlets, with the roots of great arms planted among them.

Nawkoo, Lyle thought.

"Nawkoo was a dream of who you might be."

Lyle extended a snake, watching the ripples travel along it like neon tsunamis. He raised a dozen at once and spread them over his head. They glittered in the night like belts of stars. His heaven— He was its lord, the maker of tides.

"Let them go crazy," the Polyp said. "Sweep the sea. It's you—your fury that churns it."

Fury, Lyle thought. *The power to create—not fictions, but life. The power to change—whatever displeased him.*

Fury, oh yes— He had that fire, and now he unleashed it. His mind whipped the snakes, reaching in all directions, laying hold of heaven. An unbending will and wild serpents— They twisted and raced like blue tornadoes, from the icy convolutions of the western coast to the dripping caverns that hived the east. He was the wellspring, author of currents, and all the peoples that thronged the sea would be judged true or false, pleasing or ugly, fit or unfit by him.

"And the distant worlds," the Polyp said, "far from heaven— Whirl the waters you're standing in, Lyle."

With a snake, Lyle stirred the sea at his feet, lifting creatures from hidden canyons.

"At your touch," the Polyp told him, "swarms will spark and ignite, and those rich in spirit will spread the glow. Every victory a fresh start, a new race. A new nation drenched in grace and harmony; a great city, ravines and towers glittering, a million minds alight.

"What will you say to them?"

"I am yours," Lyle replied.

"Whether you're rooted or drifting," the Polyp added, "common or strange— I will honor your moods, your shifting talents, your colors and clarities, your flaws and disparities—"

"I'll keep you from harm," Lyle said.

"All," the Polyp pronounced, "who are guided by these blue arms. And if you are menaced by any of your kind—"

"Your god will be wrathful," Lyle vowed. "Young without sires, dams without spawn. Brotherless sisters, husband-less wives—"

"And the enemies of heaven?" the Polyp asked.

The dark sky was suddenly brighter, flashing as if lights were being turned on and off. Without Lyle noticing, a rank of clouds had advanced. As he stood watching, a pair of Spider Legs crept from behind them. Thundering, booms and rumbling—the Legs struck the sea directly before him.

The enemies—

The clouds tore like fabric and a bolt shot through, aimed at Lyle's head. He was thrown back and blinded, joints crying, front stitched with cramps. A deafening ring filled the vault of his brain.

"The giant is struck," the Polyp said sadly.

Echoes of the crash reached Lyle's ears, grinding, exultant— The Spider Leg reappeared through the tear, crackling excitedly, signaling its brothers. Lyle reeled through the water, shrinking back. No shelter, no cover—

White legs rose above the ramparts of cloud, a gang of them, feeling forward. Together they thrust, piercing Lyle from every angle, driving between the lax tornadoes. And then others right behind, striking him again and again.

"Giant, disciple, zealot, pawn—" The Polyp spoke as if at a distance. "Through the dazzle and smoke, the invaders strike not only you and me. They strike the cliffs and the sea. Our magnificent picture—"

The fierce jolts continued without pause. Lyle was hunched and shuddering, trying to hang on to the realm they ruled, and the thoughts in his mind.

"The mirror of heaven is spidered with cracks," the Polyp said. "The electric stabs drive the bright fragments apart. Our glories are shattered, our image no longer intact. An intricate puzzle falling to pieces—

"A grotto. A submarine garden. A fragment of night with a sprinkle of stars. A shard of the teeming city— Through the gaps in the mirror, the seas are draining."

"Help me," Lyle pleaded.

"For this dream," the Polyp replied, "time has been elastic. But I've stretched it to the limit. Close your eyes, Lyle. Close your eyes.

"I'll retard the flow and let heaven pass slowly.

"In meandering rivers, the waters run north, seeking sounder blue islands, sounder blue coasts. Currents that are hopeful, twisting and winding, surging at the prospects before them. Currents that sound at an increasing distance.

"You can still hear the sea in my voice. With its gentle rhythm, the waters mull and subside, mull and subside."

The blue was leaving him. Lyle felt his heart emptying.

"Creation is the struggle for heaven," the Polyp said. "Not heaven itself. Clouds, rain, rivers and clouds—an ideal cycle. Pure, but lifeless. It is the minerals that bring water to life. Prisons and poisons, silicas and salts. That's why I sought you in a fallen world.

"You can feel my breath. It's cool, wind mixed with water. A lilting breeze—

"The liquid has reached your knees.

"A leaden cumulus is directly overhead. And now—

"The long cloud moves aside. A full moon, round and white.

"Shallows, shallows— Barely enough water to— Kneel down, stretch out."

The Polyp was doleful, his words halting.

"You're smaller," he said. "A man once again." Then, with remorse, "I'm going to translate this for you.

"There's a smooth surface beneath you. You're naked, on

183

a beach, with your back to the sand and the moon's light all around. A skim of water laces your thighs, whispering, cooling. It retreats, and when it returns, the foam barely touches your feet.

"And now—

"The sea is gone. Everything is still."

The Polyp paused to gather his thoughts, or perhaps to calm them.

"Dig your fingers into the sand, Lyle. Can you hear the grains squeal? Turn onto your side.

"It isn't sand beneath you. It's salt. You're on a white target of borate.

"Now raise your head. In the ghostly light, a desert appears, spreading as far as your eyes can reach.

"Above you, through the Moonhole, a pale smoke is emerging."

11   These Arms

The darkness around Lyle wasn't the darkness of night. He was in a black tent, and at the peak of the tent was a circle of white—a nozzle from which some kind of gas was emerging.

A woman's voice reached him.

There was a pane in the tent wall, and a face was framed in it. A nurse's face.

"Yes, conscious," the nurse barked into her tuner. Her tone was urgent.

As she moved away, Lyle could see chromed equipment, a cart with supplies, another nurse and a medic hurrying toward him.

The jet of gas stopped, and a leaden cover slid over the Moonhole. The tent was opening. For a moment, the daylight was too bright. Then he could see—

He was on a bed beneath white sheets. The medic stood beside him with his hand on a control panel. The nurse moved closer, gathering the folds of the tent, drawing them back. The room was small. Stiff drapes hung on either side of a window, and through the dusty glass Lyle could see a labyrinth of white buildings, walls crusted with salt, shimmering in the midday heat. Beyond the city, the remains of a prehistoric sea stretched to the horizon.

The door of the ward room sprang open, and the nurse by the door stepped aside, making way for the group filing through. There were seven. Doctor Wentt in her white coat, four men in military garb, Minister Audrie and Jordan. The Minister wore a dark suit. His eyes were on the medic, then Wentt, avoiding Lyle. The seven surrounded the bed, soldiers on the left, Wentt and Audrie on the right. Jordan stood beside the Minister.

"You've come back," Wentt said, straightening her braid over her shoulder, as if she meant to look good for the occasion. She consulted a digital tablet and began to read.

Audrie stared at his hands. The others regarded Lyle with curiosity or suspicion, seeing the vandal who defaced the patriarch—the young man who was pulled from the spire unconscious, half-dead perhaps, and carried here. He lay on this bed while the Helpers came and went, lost in his dream of heaven.

"—a serious crime," Wentt was saying, "but the State will consider the circumstances. Everything depends on your candor and willingness, your interest in making amends—"

Words, Lyle thought, she had spoken many times before.

He raised his shoulders. When he tried to shift his left arm to support his weight, it stopped short with a rattle. There was a manacle on his wrist, secured by a chain to the wall. He turned to look at the four in uniform, sensing a stiffness around his head. He was bandaged to the chin. He could feel the cables attached to his temple and the back of his neck.

Wentt had finished her preamble.

Lyle looked at Audrie. "Is my father alright?"

The Minister shook his head, refusing to answer.

"Where is he?" Lyle said lowly.

"One of many puzzled by your conduct," Wentt replied, motioning to a man in uniform. "This will be covered."

The man in uniform stepped forward. Beneath the white visor, his eyes were dark, his hair jet black. His face was frightfully narrow, as if his head had been crushed between two blocks of salt.

"Your case has been reviewed," Wentt told Lyle, "and treatments prescribed. Certain potential leniencies have been proposed, based on the outcome of this interview."

As she spoke, a pair of cameras descended down from the ceiling, rotating silently. Recessed lights brightened as the lenses found their angles.

"I'm going to ask you some questions," the narrow face said, opening a portfolio.

A Security agent.

"There is no time pressure. We are interested in whatever detail you would like to provide."

187

Somewhere a crew was hunched over a console, recording raw footage. It would be scrubbed, polished and dubbed for broadcast online. This was Expiation.

"The idea of damaging the monument—where did that come from?"

Lyle stared at the man.

"Did someone suggest it?" the agent asked.

"The idea was my own," Lyle said. "A way of expressing contempt."

"Contempt?"

"Yes," Lyle said to the cameras. "I despise the State."

Audrie's lips parted, but not to speak. He seemed to be struggling for breath. He was vulnerable—his protégé was center stage.

"You know better?" the agent continued.

"I do." Lyle drew himself up, feeling the cables tug at his head. "I'm hoarse," he complained. "Whatever you've done—" He raised his left arm to wave the man closer, but the chain stopped him.

"No sudden movements," the agent warned. He nodded to one of the other uniformed men and took a step, approaching the bed. The cameras crept forward.

Don't miss a word, Lyle thought.

"I'm inspired," he said. "By a god."

"What god is this?" the agent asked.

"The one who's going to turn this desert into a sea."

The agent glanced at Wentt. She looked surprised.

"Others share this belief?" the agent asked.

"There may be others." Lyle scanned the lenses and faces. "Do you dream of heaven?"

"We all have dreams," the agent observed.

"You know him well?" Wentt said, stepping forward. Her face was lined with concern, as if he was a patient with an unexpected ailment.

"My god is the soul of life and motion," Lyle told her. "His mind stirs the inert. When his rivers are flowing, they bring beauty and music."

At the word "flowing," Audrie met Lyle's gaze. With all his iniquity, he knew Lyle's heart. The sea, the sea— Always the sea.

"He's a creator," Lyle said. "A sculptor, like myself."

"I should have known," Wentt said. "A sculptor." She reached for his right hand, still hidden beneath the bedding, as if she meant to clasp it. At the same time, she nodded at the cameras.

His right hand—

He drew it from beneath the sheets. Out of the corner of his eye, he saw Audrie go pale. Lyle lifted his arm— It ended at the wrist. The stump was bound with white bandages.

He saw his shock mirrored in Jordan's eyes. The soldier's chin twitched and his lips were wide. Wentt stared at the stump, nostrils snagged deeply, as if she could smell the wound.

Lyle tried to rise. His legs were strapped to the bed. He struggled to free himself, but his arm was useless without— The hand that destroyed the patriarch's face. The hand the State's Saw had taken away.

189

Wentt grabbed his wrist. A fierce pain shot up Lyle's arm. She was shaking it for the cameras. "Your god," she prompted. "Tell us, tell us—"

"He's going to drown you," Lyle choked. "He's—"

"Louder, louder!"

"He'll destroy you," Lyle threatened the faces. "Every last one of you. He's going to sweep your sick world away."

Wentt signaled the agent, who turned to the control panel beside him.

A white bolt crashed into Lyle's temple, convulsing his frame. The dream circuits shorted, his memory shrank. Wentt nodded, ordering another.

Crackling, stitches, the sudden stroke— Lyle's mind reeled. The Spider Legs struck again and again. Pathways jammed, forebrain pursed, the Polyp withering—

"We can't hear you," Wentt said.

Lyle's tongue knotted, his mind had seized. *It would shatter you*, Blednishev said. The rushed journey, the union—

Crashing, crashing— The noise in his skull was like the sound of breakers, the rumble and roar of torrents racing through him. And then—the most glorious feeling: a squirming, cold and familiar. Beneath his bandages, Lyle felt an eel sneak from the hinge of his jaw.

"Enough?" Wentt crowed.

A snake uncoiled behind Lyle's ear. Others jabbed from his nape and the top of his neck. The Spider Legs were striking, but he no longer felt them.

"Have your delusions—"

190

Lyle's left wrist swelled and the manacle burst. The bandages split down his front, the leg straps snapped. As he leaned forward, he grew, overtopping those now standing mute around the bed. Before the agent could move, a blue snake reached out and cinched his thigh. Another grabbed Wentt's braid, binding it tightly.

Audrie's jaw dropped. Shock, recognition—Lyle's sea fantasy come to life. His cheeks hollowed with terror.

"Do something," Wentt urged the men in uniform.

Snakes swarmed over the mattress toward her, lashing an arm and a thigh— The sheets fell from around him as Lyle rose from the bed, baring the red stripes that banded his chest.

"I can smell you, taste you," he drew Wentt closer. "I know what you are." An eel circled her waist, another her neck. Her nose touched his—

Cries, shouts, equipment toppling. Audrie raced from the room, following the nurses and medic and the three uniformed men Lyle hadn't yet reached. Jordan remained, barking into his tuner. Weapons, battalions, urgent help needed—

With two snakes, Lyle tore the tubes and cables away,

expanding, he was rising on massive legs. His shoulders met the ceiling and cracked it. A dead agent was hanging before him, bound by a giant arm. Lyle hurled his body through the window.

Wentt was gasping and turning blue. Lyle lashed another snake around her middle, raising her, peering in her eyes as he squeezed. Guilt, sorrow, pity— Was there any recognition?

He squeezed and squeezed until every rib snapped, and the noxious insides burst from her white coat. Nothing, not even fear— She was stony as a scourge.

He hurled her after the agent. Beyond the glass teeth, picket birds had perched on the balcony railings. As Wentt flew through the hole, they dove for the pieces.

Only Jordan remained. He stood riveted, bone white, a signaler chirping on his hip. Lyle's arms whipped across the floor like the tails of tyrant lizards, circling him, binding his legs and chest, dashing his hat off and grabbing his hair.

Sirens. The echo of the State's broadcast rose from the street. The rumble of security doors closing on every floor.

"You can't breathe or speak," Lyle said, "but I know what you're thinking. One question," he offered, "before I break you in two."

"Why are you here?" Jordan asked.

"To destroy you." Lyle shook him, expecting his neck to crack.

"Heaven," Jordan murmured.

He remembers the young sculptor, a gentle voice said.

The Polyp was speaking. Lyle could feel him shifting on his throne.

"What did you say?" Lyle asked the soldier.

"The sea," Jordan gasped.

He's a child to you now, the Polyp said.

Loyal to the State, Lyle thought. Blind to its purpose. My blood is red.

Some of it is blue, the Polyp reminded him. *I'm the loftiest part of you, and nothing will harden me. Softer*, the Polyp said. *Be softer for me.*

They're everywhere, Lyle replied.

Mixed with the salt, the god said. *But not all are mites. One by one.*

Lyle felt a tremor in his brow and a throb behind his nose. Liquid seeped onto the back of his tongue.

With his eyes on Jordan, he touched the tip of an arm to the fluid and waved it before him. "A world of wonder?"

Let's give him a chance, the Polyp said.

Lyle circled a quartet of snakes and bound Jordan's head. "Would it please you," he said, "to be fit for the sea?"

He contained Jordan's struggles, cradling his brain. Sensing the circuits, searching the tangled branches. Numbness, indifference. Here, right here—

That's the place, the Polyp agreed.

The quartet of arms tipped Jordan's skull, two more spread the shell of his ear. Lyle raised a snake with a narrow taper, remembering the moment years before, when he made

arm over the canal and brought its wetted tip down.

"I'm making a change," Lyle said.

The tympanum was pierced and the taper slid in, opening a passage to the young man's mind.

Rich Shapero's stories plunge readers into unseen worlds. His previous titles, *The Hope We Seek*, *Too Far* and *Wild Animus*, combine book, music and visual art and are also available as immersive story experiences on tablets and phones. *The Village Voice* hailed *The Hope We Seek* as "a delirious fusion of fiction, music and art," and Howard Frank Mosher called him "a spellbinding storyteller." He lives with his wife and daughters in the Santa Cruz Mountains.